MW01235678

Finding Faith

Also by Dixie Land

Serenity
Return to Serenity
Exit Wounds
Circle of Secrets
Promises to Keep
Second Chances
Grave Secrets

Coming soon
Deadly Company

Finding Faith

DIXIE LAND

Published by Alabaster Book Publishing
North Carolina

Published by Alabaster Book Publishing
P.O. Box 401
Kernersville, North Carolina 27285

Book design by
D.L.Shaffer
Cover art by Janice Plonski-Beihoff

Second Edition

ISBN 13: 97809725031-3-6
ISBN 10: 09768108-0-8

Library of Congress Control
Number: 2005904085

Dedication

To Jane and Ken for all the
possibilities you gave me.

Acknowledgments

Thanks to:
My wonderful family. My husband, Larry, son Brad and daughter-in-law, Diane. Also, my three young inspirations, Alex, Ross and Ryan. I love you all very much.

My terrific writers group friends, Dave Shaffer, Lynette Hall Hampton, Joanne Clarey, Kathy Fisher, John Staples, D.E. Joyner, Helen Goodman, James Isley, Karen Fritz and Harol Marshall.

Special thanks to attorney William Causey, for answering my legal questions.

Margene Wilkins was a great help in providing answers to some of my questions on religion.

Artist Janice Plonski-Beihoff; What a gorgeous cover!

Special thanks to my business partner and friend Dave Shaffer and his wife Mary. You are great to work with and cherished friends!

CHAPTER 1

He was tall and lean but well muscled, and he carried himself with confidence. His hair was silver, his eyes a bright, sapphire blue. His richly tanned skin suggested he spent a good deal of time outdoors. As his eyes met Rachel's, he smiled warmly. He made a very handsome package.

Rachel Inman's breath caught in her throat as she stepped around her desk and met him half way.

"I'm Oliver Hargrave, and you must be Rachel," he said, extending his hand to her. "I recognize you from Fran Thompson's description."

She felt a little flutter in her stomach as their hands touched. He was even more handsome than the newspaper pictures she had seen of him. *So this is the Hargrave of Hargrave, Taylor and Thompson, the most prestigious advertising agency in the city.*

Fran, the wife of one of Oliver's business partners, had sent him to her to get some help decorating his newly purchased home in elite Cayman Shores. It was one of the many things Fran had done, and would do, for Rachel.

"Won't you have a seat?" she asked, motioning toward one of the forest green wingback chairs that faced her desk.

A short, dark-haired woman, one of Rachel's two assistants, came through a door at the back of the shop.

"Rachel," she began. "Oh, excuse me. I didn't realize you were with a client."

"Not a problem. Linda, this is Oliver Hargrave." And, turning to Oliver, "My associate, Linda Hart."

Linda greeted him then stepped to her desk and picked up her briefcase. "If you'll excuse me, I'm late for an appointment. I'll talk with you later, Rachel. Nice meeting you, Mr. Hargrave." The bell over the door jangled as it closed behind Linda.

Rachel returned her attention to Oliver. "I understand you've purchased a new home in Cayman Shores and would like a little help decorating it."

Oliver laughed, "That's an understatement. Fran thinks I need a lot of help. She thinks I need you to decorate the entire house. I'm not good at that kind of stuff, wouldn't know where to begin. My late wife took care of all that. I guess it's a woman thing." He smiled. "According to Fran, you're the best that money can buy." He flushed a little as he quickly added, "The best decorator."

Rachel laughed. "I appreciate Fran's referral. I'd love to work with you, Mr. Hargrave."

"Please. Call me Oliver. But I don't know what help I'd be."

Rachel leaned back in her tan, leather chair. "Oliver, let me explain how I like to work with my clients. I like to get to know them, their interests, favorite colors, hobbies, their lifestyles. That helps me create just the right ambience, one that fits you and your needs."

"Makes a lot of sense," he said, with a nod.

Rachel opened a desk drawer and removed a leather-bound notebook. "I'd like to start by asking you some questions and making notes, if that's okay with you, Oliver."

"Fire away," he said, leaning back in his chair and propping his right calf over his left knee.

Some twenty minutes later, they concluded. "What we need to do next is set up a time for me to go through the house, take measurements, and see exactly what we're dealing with layout wise. Have you moved in yet?"

"No. I've been renting a furnished condominium from a friend since shortly after my wife died. My daughter, Mary Jane, and her husband Brad decided to move into our family home. I didn't need the space, and they did with two little boys and a third on the way. I really hadn't planned on buying a home again, just thought I'd settle for a condo when the right one came along. I really hadn't even been looking. Then a friend from All South Realty called one day and said she'd heard about 'a house I just had to see.' Said it was perfect for me. Funny, she didn't even have the listing. She's strictly commercial management. Anyway, I made arrangements to see it and signed a contract that night."

He laughed, "I'm not usually this talkative. What you need to know is when you can see my home. When does it fit your schedule?"

Rachel couldn't repress a smile as she checked her appointment book. "I could go tomorrow afternoon. Do you have an extra key? I'll need to have access as I find pieces I think will fit, particularly when we get to the wall appointments. I also like to take the paint and wallpaper samples into the home to see how they look. The amount of sunlight, the layout of the rooms, the flow of the floor plan, all kinds of factors enter into how color appears in a home."

Oliver stood, reached into the pocket of his trousers and removed his key ring. "You may keep this one," he said, removing a key from the ring and handing it to Rachel. She tagged it with Oliver's name then placed it in her center desk drawer.

"I've enjoyed meeting you, Miss Inman. I think Fran was right about you. You're very thorough." He turned to leave but stopped and turned back to Rachel. "Here, let me give you my card. There are several numbers on it in case you need to reach me when I'm not at the office."

She smiled at him. "Thank you, Mr. Hargrave. I look forward to working with you."

Oliver Hargrave turned and started toward the front door. He stopped midway and faced Rachel. Their eyes met and locked for a moment. "Why don't I meet you at the house tomorrow. What time do you plan to be there?"

Rachel felt her pulse quicken, then a little fluttering sensation in the pit of her stomach. "Let's say around 2:00 p.m. Will that suit your schedule?"

"I'll arrange it. Until tomorrow." He turned and left her shop.

Rachel smiled to herself. *Oliver Hargrave. Quite impressive,* she thought. She had read about him in the social columns of the Journal on numerous occasions. He and his late wife, Jane, had been very active in community affairs. Then several years ago, Jane was diagnosed with cancer. She had had exploratory surgery. They found that the cancer had spread extensively. They hadn't given her much hope. After undergoing unsuccessful chemotherapy, Jane died within nine months of the diagnosis. According to Fran, they had been very devoted to one another. Oliver had had a very difficult time coping with her death.

The Thompsons had been so pleased when Oliver bought the new home in Cayman Shores. They felt that at age fifty-three, he needed more in his life than his work. "Perhaps living on the golf course will get him back into the social swing a bit too," had been Fran's exact words.

Rachel was grateful to Fran Thompson. She had sent Rachel several new clients since she had decorated the Thompson's home. And she and Fran had become friends.

Yes. Rachel's instincts had certainly been right in locating her new business where she did a little over two years ago, here on Stratford Road near Country Club Road. Though the rent was steep for a single-income, fledgling entrepreneur, it had proved a very wise choice. It took nearly two months after hanging out her shingle to sign her first client. But the day she signed the contract with Mrs. Ashcroft Craven had indeed been a lucky one for Rachel. Upon completion of the project, she had been blessed to receive three referrals, Fran Thompson being one, and a generous bonus to boot.

Within eighteen months, she needed an associate to share the workload. After interviewing several applicants, she hired Linda Hart. It had been a good decision; they worked well together from the onset. Three months later, Rachel stopped using sub-contractors and engaged Ron Jefferson to head up the installations. And now, the business was about to outgrow the three of them. Rachel knew she would soon have to add another interior designer to her staff.

She glanced at the gold wall clock. It was 4:40. There was nothing else on her schedule for today. She removed her handbag from a file drawer, locked her office and went around back to her silver Oldsmobile. She would spend the evening relaxing and going over her notes on Oliver Hargrave. Then, once she saw his new home, she'd be ready to begin her quest to find just the right pieces to fit his "retreat" as she liked to think of one's home.

Faith was a bit surprised at her eagerness to begin working with this man. She was also a bit amused at herself. She had just done something she'd never done before. She had moved a new client's home ahead of two other projects.

CHAPTER 2

Rachel's alarm buzzed at six-thirty the following morning. She liked to allow herself two punches on the snooze alarm followed by two-and a-half-hours to shower, dress and read the Journal. She also liked to eat a leisurely breakfast as she went over her schedule for the day before she left for the shop.

She tried on two outfits before deciding on a black turtleneck sweater, long, straight red and black plaid wool skirt and red blazer. She sank into the flowered, lavender comforter on her bed as she pulled on a pair of mid-calf, black leather boots. She walked across the room to look in the cheval. She was pleased. This would do nicely for a day in early November. At 9:15, she left her townhouse and drove to her shop. She arrived at precisely 9:30, unlocked the front door and turned on the lights. Linda and her other assistant, Ron Jefferson arrived at ten.

The morning was busy, but Rachel found herself glancing at her watch frequently.

As twelve o'clock approached, she felt butterflies begin to flutter in her stomach. Whenever she'd thought of Oliver Hargrave since meeting him, she had the same reaction. *"What is the matter with you, Rachel?"* she asked herself. *"You're acting like a giddy teenager."*

With that thought, Oliver's face flashed in her mind's eye again. *Why are you doing this? Why are you thinking about him so much? So what if he is charming and handsome, too? You don't even know him and, besides, he's much older than you, even if he doesn't seem it. A man like Oliver Hargrave probably has lots of women chasing after him.* With that she forced her attention back to the wallpaper selections she was making for another client and didn't allow herself to look at her watch again.

At one-fifteen the phone rang. Linda answered it.

"Rachel, it's for you. It's Mr. Hargrave."

She lifted the receiver. "Yes, Oliver. This is Rachel."

"Something unavoidable has come up. I'm not going to be able to meet you this afternoon. I'm sorry. Security knows you're coming, so you shouldn't have any problems at the gate."

"I understand. Thank you for calling." They hung up.

Rachel felt disappointed. *"Stop being foolish! He isn't interested."* she chided.

She left the shop in time to pick up a Krispy Kreme donut and soft drink for the trip. She headed west on I-40. Cayman Shores was one of the newer subdivisions in the area. Once the golf course was in and the lake had been filled, the beautiful lots had sold quickly, as one of the most respected builders in the Triad had engineered the entire project. His homes were well-designed and had a reputation of being quality from roof to basement. No two homes could be alike; architectural plans had rigid requirements and had to be submitted to a committee for approval prior to building. Now there was talk of a second golf course and a second stage of development on the additional land the developer had recently purchased.

It was a few minutes after two when she pulled up to the guardhouse at the entrance to Cayman Shores.

"Miss Inman." The guard seemed pleased to see her as he greeted her. Rachel had several clients in the exclusive neighborhood, and he was the same gentleman who'd been on duty when she had been there previously.

"Thanks." She took the pass from him and laid it on the dash of her car. She drove on through the security gates and found Oliver Hargrave's home.

It was impressive in appearance, a brick, one-story house with French Provincial roofline. The lot was small but tastefully landscaped. The home was situated with a view of the twelfth green from the lanai. Oliver had told her those had been two of its selling points for him. Rachel reached into her purse for the key, inserted it into the keyhole and let herself in.

The foyer was large and open; the home had a spacious feel from the moment she stepped inside. She went from room to room taking measurements and jotting them down. She ended up in the master bedroom. Rachel stepped inside and walked down the short privacy corridor. The expansive room had a beautiful hand-painted tray ceiling and Florida-style sitting room at the far end. Walking back into the sleeping area, she crossed into the dressing room with walk-in his and her closets. A Jacuzzi garden tub sat at one end of the bathroom, and a corner shower filled the opposite end. Broad marble vanities and a lighted wall mirror completed the space between. What a pleasure this house would be to work with, so light and open with skylights in several of the rooms. It had a wonderful flow.

As she stepped out of the bathroom, she was startled by a banging sound that seemed to be coming from the other end of the house. Had she left a door ajar? She didn't think so. For a moment she froze. Then slowly, she walked down the bedroom corridor toward the hall. She hesitated again, she heard footsteps approaching—then a voice.

"Hello? ... Hello? ... Rachel?"

She peered around the corner of the door and saw a man coming toward her. "Oh Oliver, you startled me. I didn't expect you." She laughed a little nervously.

"I did my best to finish up early. I thought you might have some questions for me. You know, about my lifestyle or some such." He said it teasingly with a broad smile on his handsome face.

"I'm glad you came. I've just finished taking all of the measurements," She returned his smile, suddenly flushing. "This is a wonderful home. I'll love working with you on it. Tell me, how do you want to feel when you walk inside and close the door? What do you want your friends to feel when they step into your retreat?"

He smiled at her again and looked into her eyes as he spoke. "Contentment, relaxation, I guess. But not so much that they don't know when it's time to go home," he added with a chuckle.

Rachel couldn't take her eyes off Oliver. There was something about him that she found quietly strong and compelling. Something sensual in this man who was actually old enough to be her father. She felt the heat in her cheeks as her heart rate accelerated.

"I thought perhaps we should..." he began, but was interrupted by his cell phone. "Excuse me." He flipped it open. "Hello, this is Oliver Hargrave."

He was silent for a moment, listening.

Rachel walked out into the living room to allow him privacy. *Get a grip*, she chided herself. *He probably has a dozen women chasing after him. Why would he be interested in you?*

He followed her down the hall and entered the living room with the phone still at his ear. "I'll be right there, darling. We'll work this out." He flipped the phone shut. "Rachel, I hope you'll excuse me. Something urgent and personal has come up. I'm sorry this keeps happening, but I need to leave now. I'll be in touch with you later."

"I understand." She smiled to mask her disappointment.

A moment later she heard the door close and his engine revving. *"See, I told you there was someone else."* She walked to the front door, let herself out and locked the door behind her

When she stepped outside, she noticed that the sun had disappeared. The sky had clouded over, becoming gray and overcast. The gloomy afternoon seemed to mirror Rachel's sudden change in mood.

CHAPTER 3

The next day, Rachel completed the project she had been working on for the last two weeks and was ready to begin on Oliver Hargrave's home. She reviewed her notes on the measurements, transferred them to her computer and began designing room arrangements and experimenting with different color combinations. She began pouring through wallpaper books, holding paint samples up to them and made another trip to the house over the weekend.

As the new week began, she was ready to see Oliver; to show him what she'd come up with and get his thoughts on her general plans before she proceeded any further. She reached him at his office Monday afternoon. His secretary answered and asked Rachel to hold for a minute.

"Hello, Rachel," he said when he picked up. "I've been meaning to call you. I've been out of town for a few days. I wanted to apologize for rushing off so abruptly last week. I feel I owe you an explanation."

"There's no explanation necessary. I understood, Mr. Hargrave."

"Oliver," he reminded her.

"Oliver." She repeated, and felt her pulse quicken. She cleared her throat; "I have some sketches ready to show you and some paint and wallpaper samples. When would it be convenient for you to meet with me?"

"Are you free this evening? If so, why don't we discuss it over dinner? Do you like Nobles?"

"I haven't eaten there, but I'm sure I would." Nobles had the reputation of being one of the finest restaurants in the entire Triad area.

"I'll make a reservation for eight, if that suits you."

"Eight will be perfect," she heard herself say.

Rachel chose a sleek, long-sleeved, black cashmere dress with a turtleneck for their dinner meeting. Oliver called for her at seven-forty. "You look very elegant this evening," he told her when she opened the door to greet him.

"Thank you." She thought he looked wonderful in his charcoal gray cashmere jacket, light gray slacks and white turtleneck but refrained from telling him.

She lifted her white jeweled sweater-coat from the arm of the chair. Oliver reached out, took it from her and slipped it around her shoulders. She found the touch of his hands unsettling.

Once in his car, Rachel felt a bit more comfortable. They chatted as they drove to Nobles. The hostess greeted Oliver by name.

"I reserved your favorite table for you, Mr. Hargrave." She lead them toward the back of the dining room. Oliver bantered with her as they walked. He obviously had been here many times and knew the young woman.

Rachel loved the feel of Old-World charm that enveloped her as she followed the hostess to their table. The high ceilings, glassed walls and white table linens gave the restaurant a sense of pristine elegance.

When they reached the table, Oliver introduced Rachel.

"We're happy to have you with us, Miss Inman," Heather said graciously.

"Thank you, Heather." They sat down and the hostess left.

Conversation, mostly small talk, flowed smoothly throughout dinner. Since Rachel hadn't been there before, Oliver recommended his favorites. For their first course they had fried oyster salad with Asian greens and creamy bacon vinaigrette, then their grilled Long Island duck breast arrived, with raspberry red wine glaze and garlic mashed potatoes. For their dinner wine, he chose Duckhorn Merlot. She wasn't disappointed; everything was scrumptious. The homemade raisin bread pudding put the crowning touch on a perfect meal.

When Oliver finished eating, he leaned back in his chair. "Now, about last week when I left so abruptly," he began. "I had to find Jillian."

So that was her name.

"Jillian is my free spirit—my youngest daughter. I absolutely adore her, but she's quite a worry to her sister and me. I don't know how two girls brought up by the same mother and father can be so different. Mary Jane is responsible, nurturing; I always knew she'd make a great wife and mom. Jillian, on the other hand, sees none of that in her future. I'm afraid she's a bit of a party girl. She was a late bloomer. I guess she's making up for it now." He smiled, showing even, white teeth.

"She's a second-year political science major at Carolina. Extremely book smart, barely has to crack a book to ace it, but doesn't take it as seriously as she should. Maybe Mary Jane was always too much of a mother hen to her little sister in the early years. I guess she just never grew up; I don't really have the answer." He shook his head.

"I suppose I have to shoulder some of the blame, too, for spoiling her as I did, especially since her mother's been gone. I find it hard to say no to Jillian. She looks so like her mother did at that age. Mary Jane is constantly scolding me, says I'll make her rotten. I guess she's turning out to be right."

Rachel smiled at him. "I suppose it is a tough situation."

"Anyway, last week Jillian disappeared. The girl she shares an apartment with at Carolina called to say that she'd been gone for three days. The wife of one of Jillian's professors had called the roommate. She was checking up, thought Jillian and her husband were off somewhere together. She thinks they're having an affair.

The roommate called Mary Jane; Mary Jane called me. It seems the wife was making threats. It took a few days to get it all straightened out."

Unsure of what response to make, Rachel simply smiled at him.

Oliver let the subject drop. "I was pleased when you called today and wanted to meet with me. I'd intended to ask you to have dinner with me last week when I met you out at the house, Rachel. And, not purely for business reasons."

She felt herself flush. "Oliver ...I."

He interrupted her. "Before you say anything, please hear me out. I know there's a great difference in our ages—that I'm quite possibly old enough to be ... well," he paused and chuckled. "I'm much older than you are. I'll just leave it at that. But I'm very much interested in Rachel Inman, the person. When Fran suggested that I talk to you about decorating my home, I'll have to admit I didn't think much of the idea. She asked me to just meet with you once, said if I still felt the same, she wouldn't say another word about it. I must admit, that meeting did make me change my mind. I wanted your help, and I wanted to know you better. You're the first woman I've felt that way about since I lost Jane." His eyes rested squarely on hers as he finished.

"Age is irrelevant, Oliver." Her words flowed with such ease. "Had you asked me to dinner last week, I'd have accepted gladly. And, I can't think of a single person I'd rather be having dinner with this evening."

Oliver reached across the table and took Rachel's right hand. He closed both of his hands around it. It set her pulse racing again.

It was pushing one a.m. when Rachel got into her bed. She felt exhilarated. The evening had been wonderful! They had talked so easily, shared so many interests, that the age difference had disappeared as soon as he had addressed it openly. Her last thought before going to sleep had been the memory of their good night kisses. And it was her first waking thought the following morning. In fact, she seemed to have dreamed of Oliver Hargrave continually throughout the night.

CHAPTER 4

If anyone had even suggested that Rachel could fall in love at first sight, she'd have laughed and told them to have their head examined. She had dated frequently, had even become engaged briefly. Kent had been bitter when she broke it off saying that she just didn't love him enough to commit.

She had buried herself in her fledgling design business and it had prospered. She was perfectly happy. She certainly wasn't looking to meet anyone. If the right person did come along, she'd know it. He'd have to be someone very special.

After their first evening together, Oliver called her daily, and they shared dinner each evening. By week's end, Rachel knew without a doubt that she was falling in love with Oliver Hargrave. When she was with him, she felt the happiest she could remember.

He had the grace, sophistication and self-assurance of the older man, with the passion and zest for life of one much younger. In him, Rachel felt she had everything she had waited for in a lover, and more. Sometimes she wondered if she would awaken some morning to find that it had all been simply a wonderful dream.

As the weeks passed, Oliver began to accompany her more frequently on her excursions to search for his homes' furnishings. When she questioned his preferences, his stock answer became "Which do you prefer?"

The home was nearly complete. Oliver moved in the first weekend in January. That Sunday evening, Oliver and Rachel cooked dinner in his new kitchen.

They laughed as they worked together over the meal. As pots, pans and empty bowls began to obscure the counter-tops and sinks, Rachel looked about and giggled.

"This takes me back to my childhood days when my father and I cooked Sunday night supper for the family."

"Ouch! That stung! Comparing cooking with me to cooking with your dad " Oliver leaned down to kiss her.

"You know better than that." She gave him a seductive look. "My father is the only other man I've ever cooked with. What I was going to say was, he'd be proud of the way we're working together. He and I were constantly bumping into one another and reaching for the same utensil. He used to say, 'Rachel Faith Inman, every time I put something down you grab it and stick it in the dishwasher. Half the time, I don't even get to use it.'"

Oliver stopped chopping the vegetables he was working on for the salad. He turned toward Rachel and placed his hands on her shoulders. "Faith. Your middle name.

I like it. It suits you. You are a Faith. You've restored my faith that great happiness is possible again after great loss. From now on, I'd like to call you Faith."

Rachel felt moisture welling in her eyes. Faith was what her favorite grandmother had called her.

The elderly woman had loved the name. When she was confined to her bed by a stroke during the last year of her life, nine-year-old Rachel visited her daily. Sometimes she would read to Grandma Carrie. Other times, she shared the events of her school day with her. Grandma Carrie had told Rachel that she was a source of faith to her. She alone had always called the child Faith.

She wrapped her arms around Oliver's waist. "Yes. I'd like that," she whispered.

"I want you to meet my daughters. I've told them about you, how happy I am when I'm with you."

"I'd love to meet them."

"We'll start with Mary Jane. She's invited us to dinner on Tuesday. I thought I'd start you out with the easy one," he said with a chuckle. "Meeting Jillian can come a little later. We'll have to catch up with her first."

Rachel felt pleased that Oliver wanted her to meet his girls but, at the same time, a little apprehensive. After all, she was only a few months older than his oldest child. She couldn't help but wonder if they'd feel some

resentment toward her, perhaps even some competition for their father's affection.

When Oliver and Rachel arrived at Mary Jane and Brad's for dinner Tuesday, Mary Jane greeted them at the door. "Come in, if you dare!" she said laughing.

"Seriously, watch your step. We haven't picked the toys up for the night, yet."

"This is Rachel, Faith, as I call her," Oliver said, kissing his daughter on the cheek.

"I've been looking forward to meeting you, Rachel. Or do you prefer Faith?" she added. Mary Jane embraced her warmly.

"Faith is fine with me."

Oliver joined the conversation. "When I learned her middle name was Faith, I thought it fit her so perfectly that from now on, she's Faith to me."

"Well, then, I guess it's Faith to us, too. Please, come in and make yourself at home." She turned, and they followed her into the den. Mary Jane was tall and slender. Her short, strawberry-blond hair appeared to Faith, to have natural curl. Had Oliver not mentioned that she was pregnant, Faith would never have guessed it, as her figure gave no hint of the coming event.

Their home was a large, two-story, southern colonial. There was a feeling of comfort about it, a look of love and belonging, with photos of family and art work obviously done by the children, lining the walls and table tops. It looked well lived-in, too, with toys scattered all about the carpet and furniture. This, combined with the

delicious aroma of dinner drifting in from the kitchen, reminded Faith of her own childhood, and she felt immediately at home.

"Oh! It's even worse in here than I thought," Mary Jane said, brushing aside some of the toys and books to make room for them to sit. "Perhaps we should go into the living room instead."

"Papa! Papa!" Two little blond boys bounded into the room and threw their arms about Oliver with such enthusiasm that Oliver nearly lost his balance.

He leaned down and hugged them both to him, laughing, as they planted kisses on his cheeks. Seeing the obvious love between the three warmed Faith's heart.

"How are my boys?" Oliver asked, returning their kisses. "Grant, Christian, I have a very special lady I want you to meet." He stood and looked at Faith. "This is Miss Inman."

Faith smiled at the boys. She leaned down and reached out to them.

"Hello, Miss Inman," Grant said, taking one of Faith's hands. The phrase was repeated immediately by the younger Christian, as he took her other hand.

Faith looked at Mary Jane. "If you don't object, I'd love for them to call me Faith."

"It's fine by me," their mother replied.

They heard the back door open, and a moment later Brad joined them. He was very tall, perhaps 6'4", with broad shoulders and a trim waist. His hair was dark brown with a generous sprinkling of gray giving him a very distinguished appearance. His skin looked as tanned

as Oliver's. He greeted his wife with a kiss and his boys with hugs. After the introductions were finished, the boys sat down on the sofa, one on either side of Faith.

Faith found them endearing children. They were warm, intelligent and beautiful to look at. Grant, the oldest, resembled his mother. He was tall for his seven years, had large blue eyes, fair skin and fine features. He had the most remarkable vocabulary Faith had ever experienced in a child of that age. Christian resembled his father. His hair was a darker blond and he was built a bit more muscularly than his older brother. He had an easy, outgoing nature and a ready smile that frequently crinkled his twinkling blue eyes nearly shut. In fact, both boys had inherited their father's blue eyes, and Christian was tall for his age, too. Christian, like Grant, was a talker, and the two spent a good bit of the evening vying for Faith's attention.

The evening went beautifully. By the end of the first hour, Faith felt like an old family friend. Dinner was homemade bread and a pot roast cooked with vegetables that tasted as good as the aroma that greeted them when they arrived.

As the evening neared an end, Faith found herself nestled between Grant and Christian on the sofa, reading a few pages from a Harry Potter book. As she read, the children snuggled closer and closer.

Mary Jane glanced over at them. "Boys, you need to give Faith a little breathing room," she chided them.

"They're fine. And I love snuggling," Faith assured her.

It was pushing ten when the boys finally scurried off to bed, still chattering away as they climbed the stairs. Soon after, Oliver and Brad went to get the coats from the entry closet.

Mary Jane turned to Faith. "I want to thank you for the change you've made in Dad's life. I haven't seen him this happy and relaxed since before Mom got sick."

"He's changed mine, too. He's a wonderful man, Mary Jane. It's been a lovely evening. Thanks for making me feel so at home with all of you."

"Brad and I've thoroughly enjoyed having you over, and there's no question as to the boys' feelings. You're a hit!"

The men returned, and a few minutes later Oliver and Faith were in his car heading home. "This was a wonderful evening, Oliver. Your daughter's terrific; the whole family is."

"You won a couple of fans in Mary Jane and Brad. And the boys! They really took to you. Maybe I should be jealous," he teased. "Four down, one to go. I spoke with Jillian this morning and arranged to meet her for lunch in Chapel Hill on Friday. I know I should have checked with you first, but I was on the phone with her and it came up. I hope that's okay. If not, we can reschedule."

"You're in luck this time. I can." She had been in the habit of making her Fridays light days for the past month, as had Oliver, so that they might spend a longer weekend together.

Meeting Mary Jane and Brad had been such a pleasant experience, that Faith, as she was now called, began looking forward to their lunch date with Jillian on Friday.

Nothing could have prepared her for the reception she would receive from Oliver's youngest daughter!

CHAPTER 5

On Friday, Faith phoned Oliver at his office at twelve fifteen to let him know she was ready to leave whenever he was.

"I'll be there is ten minutes," he told her. He made it in eight.

They reached Chapel Hill an hour and fifteen minutes later and drove directly to the restaurant, McAlisters. Jillian hadn't arrived yet. Since it wasn't crowded, they were able to get a table with a clear view of the entrance. Twenty minutes later, Jillian still hadn't arrived. When the waiter stopped by their table for the third time, Oliver and Faith ordered iced tea.

"Jillian's always late," he apologized for his daughter. "I'm sorry. I thought perhaps today she'd try a little harder, but I guess old habits die hard."

The waiter brought their tea and a complementary loaf of warm Pumpernickel along with a small tub of herbal butter. It was another fifteen minutes before a tall, raven-haired young woman entered the restaurant and headed toward their table.

"There she is now. That's my Jillian. Isn't she beautiful?"

"Yes. She certainly is." Faith smiled at his fatherly pride.

"She looks so like her mother at the same age. But, as I said, Mary Jane's the one with her mother's disposition.

Before she reached them, Faith noticed Jillian's dark brown eyes. They stood out at a distance, as did her long dark hair and flawless fair complexion. Faith couldn't help but notice the number of admiring eyes turning toward the young woman. *She truly is a strikingly beautiful girl*, Faith thought as Jillian walked toward her father.

He rose before she reached him. "Daddy! I'm sorry I'm late." They embraced. Then she turned to face Faith. All the warmth that had been in her eyes for her father, had vanished.

"Darling," Oliver said to his daughter, "this is Faith Inman."

"I've been looking forward to meeting you all week, Jillian." Faith offered her hand and smiled graciously at the young woman.

Jillian took Faith's hand. Jillian's hand was cold; her grip on Faith's so tight that it was all Faith could do not to wince.

"I've been waiting to meet you, too," she said. Her tone was warm, but she gave Faith such a cold stare that it caused a chill to run through her. Jillian's back was to her father, so this reception was just woman to woman. And there was no mistaking that Faith Inman saw pure hate in Jillian Hargrave's eyes.

CHAPTER 6

As she and Oliver headed back to Winston-Salem, Faith felt sick. Lunch had been a disaster. Not that anyone on the outside would notice. Jillian had been too clever for that. It was obvious to Faith that Jillian had thought this out very carefully in order to hide it from her father. It was an exchange strictly between the two women. And she had been successful. Oliver was oblivious to it all. Faith could tell by his conversation that he hadn't a clue as to what had gone on between his daughter and herself.

During the meal, Jillian had been bubbly and talkative. Her conversation had all been directed toward her father. It was clear to see by the way that he looked at his youngest daughter that he did indeed adore this "free spirit" of his. When Faith had tried to enter in by asking the girl an occasional question, Jillian's answers had had a subtle but unmistakable curt edge to them. And those eyes! It amazed Faith that such a warm brown hue could exude such ice as they did whenever they met Faith's gaze.

When they finished eating, Faith had excused herself and had gone to the powder room. Within moments, Jillian joined her there. The one other woman washed her hands and exited.

"Just so that we're clear on things," Jillian began, right hand on her hip, "I think we should have a little talk."

Uncertain of what to expect, Faith tried to smile. "I know you met Mary Jane and her family, and that they're all quite impressed with you, but I'm not Mary Jane. And I'm not easily impressed. And I also know what you're up to. You think my father would be a 'good catch,' that he's a wealthy man. Give it up, Rachel or Faith or whatever you call yourself! Find someone your own age."

Faith's cheeks burned as she stared at Jillian in stunned silence.

"Now. Let's go back and join Daddy." She reached for the knob and held the rest-room door open. She motioned Faith to go through ahead of her. Jillian wore a warm smile as they reached Oliver at their table.

"I think lunch went well, don't you?" Oliver's voice interrupted Faith's private reflections.

"I'm not so sure about that," she said faintly.

"Nonsense! You just have to get to know Jillian. She's entirely different than Mary Jane…not nearly as open with her feelings. That's all. I think she liked you. I can't wait for you to know her better. She's a wonderful girl.

Though I must admit, she can be headstrong and difficult at times. Still, she can melt my heart with a look, always could. She needs me more than Mary Jane does."

There was absolutely no way that Faith could tell Oliver what had transpired between Jillian and her. She remained silent for most of the trip back to Winston-Salem. She would have to give this matter a good deal of thought. But, not now. She was too emotional now, too close to it all.

"Darling, are you not feeling well? You've been so quiet."

"I'm a little tired, and I have a headache."

"I think I've been keeping you too busy. Let's make it an early night.

Why don't you sleep in tomorrow? Call me when you wake up; we'll make plans for the evening if you're feeling up to it."

Back in her apartment, Faith put a load of clothes into the washer then went into the living room. She picked up the mystery novel she had purchased recently, *JILTED BY DEATH*, by Lynette Hampton. But when she looked at the title, the "Jilted" reminded her too much of Jillian, and she put the book down. She'd begin it another time when she wasn't so upset.

It bothered her that she had let the young woman get to her like this. It wasn't like her. Why hadn't she said, "Now just a darn minute!" And then told Jillian what was on her mind. But she hadn't. Jillian's attitude had taken her so by surprise that she had been speechless. And she wasn't about to make a public scene, which likely might have happened had she stood up to Jillian. She fixed herself a sandwich, poured a glass of milk and went into the living room still mumbling to herself about what she should have said.

She turned the TV on and channel surfed for a while. She found nothing of interest. When she finished eating and folding the laundry, she decided to take her shower and make it an early night. She snuggled into her bed at nine-thirty. Five minutes later the phone rang. *Probably Oliver,* she thought, *checking on me.* She reached over to her bedside table and lifted the receiver.

"Hello."

There was no answer.

"Hello," she said again.

Still, no reply.

She shrugged and hung the receiver up. She pulled the covers up around her neck and turned onto her side trying to find a comfortable position. She tossed and turned for several minutes before the phone rang again. She let it ring three times then reached for the receiver. "Hello"

There was no response. But this time, Faith heard someone breathing.

"Hello," she said in a firm voice.

There was a muffled sound on the line. She slammed the receiver down and waited a couple seconds, then lifted it again. The connection hadn't been broken, she still heard breathing. She hung up again and waited a full ten seconds. This time when she lifted the receiver, she heard a dial tone. She placed the receiver on the bedside table next to the phone. What kind of juvenile game was this? Was this Jillian's doing? She tossed and turned and argued with Jillian in dreams all night. When she woke the next morning she felt more tired and upset than when she had gone to bed the night before.

"This is ridiculous!" she said aloud. "I'm not going to live like this."

She returned the receiver to its cradle then removed a phone book from the dresser drawer. She looked up a number, lifted the receiver and dialed.

CHAPTER 7

When she finished her phone conversation, she called Oliver. She reached his answering machine and left him a message. "I'm feeling better this morning, but I have some business to tend to. I'll see you when I've finished."

She showered and dressed rapidly. She dressed in red. That's a good power color she thought as a smile crossed her lips. She went to the garage and got into her car. She started the engine and checked her gas gauge; the needle showed three-quarters full.

She got on Interstate 40 and drove east. When she was beyond Greensboro, she set her car on cruise. Some forty-five minutes later, she pulled up in front of Jillian's apartment building in Chapel Hill. She parked and locked her car. Mary Jane had assured her on the phone earlier that Jillian would still be at home, perhaps even still in bed as she and the professor had been forced to call it quits, and there was currently no man in her life. She routinely slept in on Saturdays. Faith took the stairs to the second floor, mentally rehearsing, yet again, what she would say to Jillian. When she reached the second floor, she found 6-B and rang the bell.

She waited a few seconds before ringing again. She heard stirring inside, then… "Hold on, I'm coming."

The door opened slowly and Jillian stood with a peach colored towel wrapped turban style around her head wearing a kelly-green terry-cloth bathrobe. "What are you doing here?" She appeared surprised, off guard.

"I think we need to have another little talk, Jillian. I didn't think it could wait." Today Faith was the one who had planned things out, the one in control.

Jillian opened the door wide, peered out into the hall and looked to her right, then her left.

"I've come alone, Jillian. This is between you and me."

Jillian stepped aside and Faith went into the living room. "Do you want a cup of coffee? I just made a fresh pot."

"Thanks. That would be nice." Faith followed her into the kitchen and waited until Jillian had poured their coffee and was seated at the breakfast bar. Jillian motioned her to sit, but Faith remained standing.

"You really took me by surprise yesterday, Jillian. I was so looking forward to meeting you. I'd had such a lovely evening with Mary Jane's family, and Oliver is such a gentleman that I have to admit you really threw me, to the point that I was speechless, and that is a rare occurrence for me."

As Jillian sat sipping her coffee, her eyes remained fixed on Faith.

"Yesterday, you accused me of thinking of your father as a 'good catch'," Faith continued. "Well, you are exactly right about that. He's a great catch, but not because he has money. I've worked very hard for the last six years. I put myself through school and started a business on a shoestring. I now own a very successful decorating business, and I don't need anyone else's money. I've dated men my own age who can't hold a candle to your father. In fact, I was engaged a while back, but I broke it off because there was something missing. I poured myself into my work, and that was enough for me. Then I met your father. Oliver is more than a great catch; he's a wonderful, thoughtful, caring, fun-to-be-with man, and I intend to keep seeing him. He's all and more than I ever wished for in a man. I've waited a long time to find someone like him. I love him, and he's the only one who can put an end to this relationship."

Jillian put her coffee cup down. "Did you talk to him on the way back yesterday? Does he know you came up here to see me?"

"No. This is between you and me, Jillian. Oliver thought lunch went well, and I didn't have the heart to tell him differently. He loves you very much and talked so fondly of you yesterday. I wouldn't disappoint him by telling him how you behaved toward me. No. As I said when I came, this is strictly between us."

Jillian arched her eyebrows and shrugged. She poured herself another cup of coffee and held the pot out offering Faith a refill. She declined.

"How'd you get my address?"

"Mary Jane gave it to me."

"What did you tell her?"

"That I was going to Chapel Hill and wanted to stop by your place."

"What did she say?"

"She gave me your address."

"And?"

"I'd like to be your friend, Jillian. I'm willing to forget yesterday ever happened and start fresh. It's up to you now." Faith walked over to the counter and put her cup down. "I'm sorry to come in on you unannounced, that isn't my usual style. But the last couple of days haven't exactly been usual. I wanted to talk to you, and I didn't feel it should wait. I didn't want to take the chance of calling and having you turn me down."

For the first time since Faith had met Oliver's daughter, Jillian smiled at her. "You've got guts, I'll give you that. I'll think about it. I'll let you know."

"Fair enough." Faith lifted her cup and took a few sips then walked over and poured the rest into the sink. Thanks for the coffee." She walked back through the living room and let herself out of the apartment.

Traffic was fairly heavy on the ride home. As she neared the Burlington area, traffic came to a standstill. There had been some construction at various points along the

way. Faith assumed that was probably the cause for the delay until she heard what sounded like several sirens. She glanced at her watch as she felt her stomach growl. She hadn't had much breakfast and could see an exit a few yards ahead, the last one before leaving Burlington. She maneuvered over to the shoulder of the road and took the Elon College exit.

She found a restaurant a short distance beyond, parked and went inside. The talk in the restaurant was of the twelve-car pile-up that had occurred about an hour earlier.

A traveler from the other direction who had passed by said it looked bad; ambulances had been called in from Greensboro as well as Burlington.

"You might as well take your time eating, Ma'am," he said to Faith when he learned she was traveling to Winston-Salem. "Traffic ain't goin' no place for a good while yet."

When she finished eating she decided to go on into Burlington and do a little shopping. She drove to a nearby mall. She caught snippets of conversation from other shoppers about the accident, too. An hour later, she went out to her car where she had left her cell phone. When she picked it up, she noticed she'd had a call. She cleared the phone and dialed the highway patrol to inquire about the traffic. She was told it should be moving again within twenty minutes. While she was talking with them she had a beep. She concluded with them and took the other call. It was Oliver.

"Thank God. You're not hurt, are you?" There was agitation in his voice.

"No. I'm fine."

"I've been trying to call you since I heard about that terrible accident. I called Jillian as I often do on Saturdays, and she mentioned you'd been by but had left shortly before I called. I was surprised. Later, when I turned the TV on and heard the news, I tried to reach you and couldn't. I was worried that perhaps you'd been involved."

"I'm held up in traffic, that's all. But it sounds awful from what folks around here are saying. I just spoke with the highway patrol, and they say traffic should be moving again soon."

"Faith, there's something we need to talk about. I think we need to talk tonight. Do you want to come here when you get back, or shall I meet you at your place?" Oliver sounded solemn.

Faith felt a little chill. "You sound so serious, are you going to give me a hint?"

"It is serious, but not on the phone. Why don't you come here?"

"Okay. I will."

"Be careful." He broke the connection.

What was so serious that he couldn't tell her what it was about on the phone? What had Jillian said to him when they spoke? What was the girl capable of? How far would she go to break them up? She certainly was her father's darling, but how much influence did she have on him? Faith had been feeling much better since

her talk with Jillian, now an uneasy feeling replaced that comfort.

CHAPTER 8

Faith turned into Cayman Shores forty-five minutes later. When she pulled into the semi-circular drive in front of Oliver's home, he opened the front door and met her as she got out of her car.

"You really gave me a scare this afternoon. All sorts of pictures went through my mind when I couldn't reach you. I developed a hell of a headache."

"It was a terrible accident. I'm sure there are a number of very upset people tonight. I didn't hear if there were any fatalities, did you?"

"There were five and four others are in critical condition, and a good number have minor injuries."

"Twelve cars. That could involve a lot of people."

"No names have been released."

They walked into the house and went back through the kitchen to the adjoining sitting area. Oliver picked up the remote and turned on the gas log. There was still

a chill in the air most evenings, even though they were closing in on April. Faith took a seat on the white leather sofa.

"I just mixed a pitcher of martinis. Shall I pour one for you?"

"Will I need one for this serious talk you want to have with me?"

He chuckled. "I hope not."

He poured them both a martini and dropped an olive into his, three into hers, because he knew how much she liked them.

Faith was relaxing. He certainly didn't seem at all upset with her, only relieved that she was here, safe and sound, with him. She leaned against the end sofa pillow as he handed her the martini. She took a sip. "This hits the spot."

Oliver sat down beside her, took a drink and began immediately. "Faith, it's no secret to you, or anyone else, how important you've become to me. When I lost Jane, I felt that I'd end up spending the rest of my life alone. Then we met. Fran Thompson certainly knew what she was doing when she sent me to you. At that first meeting, I became intrigued with you. You were so in control, and yet, you put me instantly at ease. I loved the way you listened and looked at me, and your smile. I loved your smile. I found it all quite enchanting. The more time I spent with you, the more I wanted to be with you. I love you more than I ever thought possible. Today frightened me. I could have lost you. I'm much older than you are, and with that age comes a little impatience.

Faith was gazing at him intently. In the flickering light of the fire, his eyes looked bright yet very intent.

He moved even closer to her before continuing. "What I'm trying to tell you is that I want to marry you, Faith Inman. And, I don't want to wait very long."

Faith put her drink down and moved into Oliver's embrace. "I want that, too, Oliver," she whispered against his cheek. "Nothing would make me happier." She looked into his blue eyes.

"Faith Hargrave," his voice sounded husky. "I like the sound of ..." Their lips met before his sentence was finished.

The next day, Oliver and Faith met Mary Jane, Brad and the boys at church. When Mass ended, Oliver shared their news. Mary Jane threw her arms around them both, and the boys joined in, laughing and shouting, "Group hug, group hug."

"Good for you!" Brad told them grinning.

"We've decided on a date; April fourteenth," Oliver told them. "I know that doesn't give us much time. But it will be simple and very small, only our families and our most intimate friends."

Mary Jane leaned toward Faith's ear, "I can't tell you how pleased I am."

"I'm so glad you feel that way. I counted on you and Brad to be accepting, but I can't help but wonder what Jillian's reaction's going to be."

"I wouldn't worry too much about Jillian," Mary Jane said. "She's a lot of talk. And she's very much wrapped up in her own situation right now."

Tuesday morning Faith arrived at her office thirty minutes later than usual. There was a note taped to her door. It was scrawled on a soiled, crinkled piece of paper. Someone had tried to deliver a package. The note said they'd try again later.

Faith didn't think much about it even though it hadn't been from UPS or FED EX. She received many parcels in her line of work. About eleven-thirty she heard the bell over her door chime. She looked up from her desk to see a messenger from one of the local novelty stores enter the shop.

"I have a delivery for Miss Faith Inman."

"I'm Miss Inman."

"Then this is for you." He handed her a thin eight by ten box, turned and exited the shop.

Faith went to her desk to open it. She was curious; she hadn't ordered anything. Who would be sending her a package via a messenger? She took a letter opener from her desk drawer and cut the tape on the end of the box. She pulled out the contents wrapped in white tissue paper. She pulled the paper back to reveal a small, white flag on a thin black stick. She read the typed note that lay beneath it. "I've thought it over. Let's call a truce." At the bottom the gift card read, "Sent by Jillian." Faith smiled. She was pleased. Fair enough, she thought, even though it had been a one-sided battle.

Faith and Oliver were true to their promise to keep the nuptials simple and intimate. Faith didn't want to leave her business associates out. And, her parents and sister flew in from Louisiana. Her brother and his family planned to drive down from Ohio the evening prior to the wedding in time to attend the rehearsal dinner. She was eager for all of them to meet Oliver.

Her mother had sounded a bit hesitant on the phone when Faith called to tell the family of their wedding plans. "But he's so much older than you, dear," she had said.

"Why, he's closer to our age than yours."

They had flown in two days before the ceremony. Oliver had charmed Carol Inman the moment they met at the airport. As the women waited while the men picked up their luggage on the lower level, Faith's sister, Nancy, said, "I don't care if he is closer to dad's age, Faith. He's hot!"

"For once, Nancy, you and I agree." They both laughed. They had argued endlessly as teenagers but were actually quite close now, even though there were miles between them. Nancy, a lab technician for a research company in Toledo, was three years younger than Faith, and still waiting for Mr. Right.

Faith's father, Mel, and Oliver found they had a good deal in common; both were in sales, loved golf, and adored Faith.

Oliver's children, his business partners and their wives, and two other close friends of Oliver's were the only others in attendance. Though Jillian was far from warm with Faith, she was more civil than she had been at their previous meeting. For that, Faith was grateful.

They had agreed on the garden at Tanglewood Park for the wedding ceremony. They wanted something simple, yet beautiful. The weather co-operated. Father Joseph officiated at the ceremony. Faith thought that without a doubt this was the happiest day of her life, one of many to come in the years ahead with this wonderful man who made her feel so very special, so complete.

A long time friend and client of Oliver's, Doug Armstrong, offered his beach home to them for their honeymoon. Faith was still feeling exhilarated when they pulled into North Myrtle Beach. She was ready for the drive to end and the honeymoon to begin.

Oliver drove on to the last beach house on the northern-most stretch of oceanfront in the secluded, single-family section of beachfront property.

She liked the warm, cozy feeling the impressive looking beach house gave her as they pulled through the latticed parking area beneath the house. It was driftwood in color with white trim. The roofline had an oriental flair, making the house look like a large Japanese pagoda. They walked up the side steps and along the wide side porch on the right of the house, then went left several yards to the front door. Faith fell in love with it. The heavy door was painted a persimmon orange and oriental symbols carved into it, added character.

"This is wonderful!" Faith said, turning to Oliver. "I can't wait to see the inside."

"I think you'll be pleased, Darling. Of course, you need to keep in mind that Doug is a bachelor."

Oliver stepped forward with the key to let them in.

Faith glanced toward the other end of the porch and noticed a carved wooden sign attached to the end rail. It read, *Summer Fling*.

"Summer Fling," Faith whispered. She felt a chill run the entire length of her spine. A pang of melancholy swept through her "I don't like that at all," her words were almost inaudible. "It sounds so very fleeting."

CHAPTER 9

Their honeymoon was wonderful! The week flew by all too quickly. They made love, walked on the beach, made love, dined out each night, golfed once, slept some and made love. Faith couldn't remember when she'd felt more fulfilled and contented.

When she awakened on the final day of their marvelous week together, she turned over to reach for Oliver. His side of the bed was empty. She rose, went to the door and stepped out of their bedroom. The aroma of fresh coffee filled her nostrils and, as she headed for the kitchen, she heard conversation. She went back for her robe and wrapped it around her before joining Oliver and his guests.

"Good morning little sleepy-head," Oliver said, as she appeared in the doorway. Come join us. I'd like for you to meet some friends of mine."

Faith ran her fingers through her sleep-tousled hair to brush it away from her face. "You'll have to excuse my appearance," she said, feeling a bit embarrassed.

"Don't apologize. You look wonderful. Darling, this is Ben Hall, his wife Kitty and their friend, Lynette Hampton. The Halls' own a place a short ways down the beach. Ben and I fish together several times a year. In fact, a few of us from the firm come down and spend a week at Doug's in the spring and fall to fish, drink a few beers and grow a beard until it's time to leave."

She tried to picture Oliver with a beard as she offered her hand to Ben who was closest. "It's nice to meet you." She took Kitty's hand then turned to Lynette. She studied her face. "You're the Lynette Hampton who writes mysteries, aren't you? I recognize you from your photo on the jacket cover."

Lynette laughed. "You've found me out."

"I'm such a fan! I have your latest, *Buried Lives*, at home ready to begin when I go back. I loved, *Jilted by Death*!"

"Thank you. It's always good to meet a fan. Better a fan than a critic." She took Faith's hand and gave her a warm smile.

Faith poured herself a cup of coffee and joined them at the table. "So, Lynette Hampton really is your name, not just a pen name."

"That's right. I want full credit." She was a striking woman with a ready smile. Her silver hair was cut in a medium-length bob. She had bright blue eyes and an easy-going nature that made Faith feel very much at ease.

Faith looked at Ben and Kitty. "I'm sorry. I don't mean to ignore you."

"No offense taken, honey." Kitty laughed. "We don't mind. She's a terrific writer, and she's earned the right to be appreciated. Lynette's a good friend, has been for years. She and I have known each other since our freshman year of college."

Two hours later, the Halls and Lynette left. Faith went into the bedroom and began packing their clothes to leave. Oliver joined her. "Gosh, I hate to give all this up and go back to the real world."

"We don't have to go if you don't want to, Mrs. Hargrave. Doug said the place was ours for three weeks, if we wanted to stay that long."

"I do have to get back, Oliver. You know Linda's already called here twice with new clients I need to see, and there are two others that I had already promised to begin projects for this coming week. It seems that since we announced I was to become Mrs. Oliver Hargrave, I'm even more popular," she winked at him. "So, you must accept some of the blame for this."

"Then back to the real world it is."

Faith noticed that he was massaging his forehead and temple above his left eye. He had done it earlier while the Halls' were here, too. "Do you have a headache, dear?" She asked as she moved toward him. She began to massage his neck and shoulders.

"I guess it's just the thought of leaving all this wonderful leisure with the woman I love and getting back to the rat race." He took her hands and pulled her around to him on the bed. She sank into his embrace.

There was no time for Faith to ease into the work week. When she arrived at the shop Monday morning, she had three messages from potential clients to contact and a full calendar for the week.

By the next month's end, Faith was silently wishing she and Oliver could return to the beach. Oliver came in on a Friday evening and delivered the good news. "Doug is selling the beach house and has recommended to the prospective buyers that you decorate it for them. I suppose we should go down and have another look. What do you think?"

"Oliver! That's wonderful news! It's absolute music to my soul."

"I suppose we ought to stay at least three or four days to let you get everything you need to do the job right." He grinned at her. "And, they've given you carte blanche. They're convinced you have impeccable taste.

"How wonderful! I'll arrange it. I think I can get away next Friday morning for a long weekend!"

"Good. Then I'll arrange that, too."

The following evening, they were invited to dinner at Mary Jane and Brad's. They rang the bell at seven-thirty, and Christian opened the door with Grant at his heels.

"I beat!" Christian cried out excitedly. "I get the first hug!"

"Not fair," Grant shouted, pushing his way toward Oliver and Faith.

"Here, here now. What's all this?" Oliver chuckled. "I see four little arms and four big ones. No one's gonna be left out."

Mary Jane rounded the corner from the den shaking her head, and holding her back with one hand and her ever expanding mid-section with the other. "They've been at one another all day. Boys, you need to go to your room and think about the talk we had just before Papa and Faith got here." The boys complied and scampered off in the direction of the stairs.

Oliver embraced his daughter. "Not feeling well, dear? You should have called. We could have all gone out. We still can."

"No, Dad, but thanks. I opened a bag of salad greens from the market and stuck some potatoes in the microwave. Brad's grilling some steaks. I'm just tired, I guess. To be honest, it's easier to stay here and eat, than it is to get everyone ready and out the door these days. I'll be glad when the next six weeks are over."

"We'll make it an early evening," Faith said, giving Mary Jane a hug. "I think we could all use one."

The evening was pleasant and, true to their word, at nine-thirty Faith and Oliver were ready to leave. "I'll just help Mary Jane carry these dishes to the kitchen and I'll be right with you, Oliver."

Oliver and Brad went into the den while Mary Jane and Faith went into the kitchen. "I've wanted to talk to you about Dad," Mary Jane confided as soon as they were out of earshot. "I was going to call you if we didn't have a chance to talk this evening. I'm concerned. He's had a lot of headaches lately. I think he needs his eyes checked. When I suggested it to him, he got a little upset with me."

"I've noticed it too, Mary Jane. He's been working some long hours lately, and there have been some pressures on him. You know, with JR Craven cutting back like they have the last few years, their ad business has slacked off considerably. Granted, they still have a great deal of High Point furniture market advertising, but it hurts to have a client as big as Craven cut back. And, there have been others, also. I know he's trying to keep his worries from me. Fran Thompson and I talked recently, and her husband is feeling the pressure, too. I think that's what the headaches are all about."

"That didn't even cross my mind, but, of course, it makes perfect sense. I thought he was just being vane about wearing glasses because he has such a young and beautiful wife," Mary Jane said with a smile. "I hate to hear that about the business, but I'm glad you told me."

On Sunday, as they were driving home from church, Oliver was very quiet. Faith looked over at him and she could tell he didn't feel well. "Another headache?"

"Yes. I'm more than ready for next Friday and a few days at the beach."

The four days at the beach were a tonic to both of them. The Halls were down from Richmond the same weekend and, one of the evenings, the foursome went to dinner at J. Edwards. It was a favorite of the Halls, even though reaching it entailed a forty-five minute drive through heavy traffic.

Oliver seemed to feel marvelous. They slept late and walked on the beach each morning and evening. He helped Faith with the measurements then went around with her to some of the area furniture stores to get some ideas of what was available locally. It was to be a complete overhaul, from carpet to paint, to wallpaper, to furniture and accessories. She had been given carte blanche on all selections within a specified budget. Working together, they accomplished a great deal in four days, even managing to squeeze in eighteen holes of golf. Faith selected the paint and wallpaper then contracted a company in North Myrtle to provide the labor. They were in luck and wouldn't have to wait long for the contractors to get started. The work was scheduled to begin the middle of the following week.

All too soon, they were headed back to Winston-Salem. Faith turned to Oliver, "I kind of wish I knew the new owner and that they might invite us to visit for a week or so once it's all finished. I have nothing but wonderful memories of *Summer Fling*." The name didn't affect her adversely at all now.

"It would be nice," Oliver agreed.

"You seem to be feeling well these days."

"I am. The headaches were nothing that a little rest and relaxation with you couldn't cure."

Faith typed up the invoice for decorating *Summer Fling* eight weeks later. She sent it to Doug as she had been instructed to do. She had made several additional trips to oversee and complete the project. To her disappointment, Oliver had been able to accompany her on only one of them. It was understandable though. Each had a demanding business to run, and Faith was hearing more and more from Fran Thompson that the ad agency was having some internal problems. And she confided to Faith that her husband, Henry, was becoming very concerned over the falling price of the company stock. Still, Oliver never mentioned a word about it. Faith found it all very upsetting, but she was reluctant to broach the topic with Oliver. He'd bring it up himself if he wanted her to know. She just wished Fran didn't go on about it whenever they talked as she found it so upsetting. Perhaps she should put an end to the conversation the next time Fran brought it up.

The summer was sweltering and July was ushered in with a torrential rainstorm. Faith was at the shop alone when the day turned black as night at three in the afternoon. The power went out. Bolts of lightening danced through the sky. They were the only illumination for nearly forty minutes. Faith usually liked a storm but not an electrical one. It unnerved her. Thankfully, as soon as the storm ended, the power was restored. Faith's phone rang.

It was Oliver. "Are you all right, Darling? I tried to call you a few minutes ago and couldn't get through."

"I'm a little shaken. That was a terrible storm. My electrical power just came back on. The phone lines must have been affected too."

"I've had a call from Brad. Mary Jane delivered a little boy just before the storm began. Mother and baby are both doing well. He was a big one, nearly ten pounds. They named him Taylor."

"That's wonderful! He really came in with flash and fanfare, didn't he?" Faith laughed.

"I thought we'd get a bite at Ryan's since we won't be too far from Coliseum Drive then go on up to the hospital this evening."

"Sounds good! I'll leave here within the hour and meet you at home whenever you can make it."

They didn't stay at the hospital long as Mary Jane was exhausted. Taylor was beautiful! Faith had never held a newborn infant before. She was very uneasy and was relieved to pass him back to his mother.

Grant and Christian could hardly contain their excitement. They had taken gifts to the hospital for their new brother. Christian was disappointed that Taylor was so oblivious to the black-and-white spotted stuffed dog, which had been his gift to his new brother. However, he had been most agreeable to taking it home and playing with it until Taylor could join them at home and claim it for his crib. Grant was feeling quite the grown-up big brother as he explained to Christian that babies "Can't do anything but get taken care of for a real long time after they get here."

When Faith and Oliver reached their home later that evening, Oliver mixed a small pitcher of martinis and poured one for each of them. "Stay here. I'll be right back." He left momentarily and went out to the garage. When he returned he had a long box in his hands. It looked like a florist's box.

Faith smiled at him as he held the box out to her. "For me? She looked surprised.

"I know it's still two days until your birthday, but I couldn't wait. Go ahead, open it." He looked like a little boy to Faith.

She lifted the lid and drew in her breath. "They're gorgeous! Crimson roses... my favorites. They look and feel like pure velvet," she said, gently touching one of the blooms. "I'd almost forgotten. I do have a birthday coming up, thirty-four."

"Look in the envelope." He watched her, still smiling.

She lifted the flap and removed the card. There was a rose on the card, the same color as the roses in the box. Inside, the card said simply, "Because I love you," in Oliver's handwriting. She opened the paper that was folded inside it and saw that it was a deed. She read it, and tears of joy filled her eyes. It was the deed to *Faith's Retreat'*.

He had bought the beach house from Doug and let her decorate it for herself. She stepped into his embrace so overcome that she could barely manage to whisper, "I love you. Thank you. I love…"

His lips covered hers before she could finish. "Happy birthday! Mrs. Hargrave. Happy birthday," he whispered in her ear.

The following Wednesday, Oliver came home from the office with a sick headache. When Faith arrived at five o'clock, he was in bed with the blinds pulled. "Eye-strain, I guess," he said. "The print was blurring badly when I tried to read some contracts today. I'm afraid old age is setting in," he said in an attempt at humor.

"I think we need to make an appointment to have your eyes checked, Oliver. I'll call someone in the morning."

Two days later, Oliver kept his appointment with ophthalmologist Kenneth Mullins. He was at the office for an hour and a half of examination and testing.

When Oliver arrived at their home afterward, Faith was waiting for him. "What did Dr. Mullins find? Are you going to be sporting a very distinguished pair of glasses soon?"

"We'll see," Oliver said. "Maybe I'll go with contacts."

Several days later, Oliver called Faith at her shop and asked her to meet him at his personal physician's office. "Can you come right over? It's in the medical park clinic off of Hawthorne, Dr. Edwin Burns." His voice sounded strained.

"Yes. Of course, I can. I'll be right there." She jotted the address down, grabbed her handbag and left a note for Linda. She locked the shop and drove to the doctor's office.

Once in the office, she stopped at the receptionist's window. "I'm Mrs. Oliver Hargrave. My husband called and asked me to meet him here."

"Yes, Mrs. Hargrave. Please have a seat. I'll let them know you've arrived."

She had barely taken a seat when a woman in uniform opened a door to her left and called her name. Faith rose and followed her down a long corridor until she stopped at a room on the right.

"They're waiting for you." The nurse knocked, then opened the door and held it for Faith.

When she stepped inside, she saw the doctor seated at his desk facing Oliver. Her husband's back was to her. Oliver turned, rose and reached his hand out for hers. "Come, Darling, have a seat. Dr. Burns wants to talk to us." Oliver's face looked ashen. His blue eyes had lost their spark.

Chapter 10

They left the doctor's office an hour later. As they began the ride home, conversation was forced as each tried to put up a brave front for the other.

"This is just a little inconvenience," Oliver began. "A bit of a setback, that's all. I'll have the biopsy, go for treatment and a few weeks later it will all be behind us."

"You're right. You're the picture of health. You exercise regularly, don't smoke, you only drink in moderation. I know this," she hesitated, reluctant to give it a name. "This will turn out to be benign, but, if it doesn't, we'll beat it."

Oliver reached for his wife's hand and gave it a little squeeze. "You're absolutely right. I'm not even going to mention it to the girls. No need to worry them now when it will all be behind us soon."

Faith felt nauseated, and her head ached terribly. She felt like crying but was determined not to give in to it.

When they reached the house, Oliver took two steaks out of the freezer and thawed them in the microwave.

"I'll stick a couple of potatoes in to bake and toss a salad," Faith said, going to the fridge. She had no appetite; she was simply going through the motions for Oliver. When the meal was ready, she had to force herself to swallow the few bites she put into her mouth. Oliver finished before she did.

"Why don't you go into the den and relax," she said. "I'll finish up and stick these dishes in the dishwasher. It won't take me long. I'll be with you in a few minutes."

As soon as she was alone, she threw the food that was left on her plate into the garbage disposal. After she had straightened the kitchen, she joined Oliver in the living room. He was rubbing his forehead as she entered the room but stopped as soon as he saw her. She walked up behind him and began to massage his head and neck. They talked very little. By ten o'clock, they were in bed.

Oliver wrapped his arms around her. Soon, she could tell by his breathing that he was asleep. Very quietly, so as not to disturb her husband, she rolled out of his embrace. She got out of their bed and went out into the den.

Alone at last, she gave in to the sobs she had fought to suppress ever since Dr. Burns had told them that he strongly suspected the tumor was malignant. They would know more in the next week after further testing. At that time, they would discuss all the options. But, Faith reminded herself, he only said suspected. That meant one could also suspect that it was benign. That was what she'd focus on. It just couldn't be happening again. They'd had so little time together, only a few months. And not after all he had gone through with Jane. No. It couldn't happen to both of them at such a young age.

"Oh, God, please let it be benign. Please God," she implored in a whisper.

Four days had passed since that "black Friday," as Faith referred to it mentally. They had an appointment to meet with an oncologist at 3:30 that afternoon. Faith had taken the day off. She planned to meet Oliver at the agency and drive with him to the doctor's office. She glanced at the mantle clock frequently as the time neared for her to leave. She had always considered herself a religious person; she had always put her trust in the Lord. But never had she been more spiritual, or prayed more fervently in her life, than she had during these last few days. And so, as she left to pick Oliver up, it was with great hope in her heart and a silent prayer on her lips.

Forty-five minutes later they sat in Dr. Carter's private office awaiting his arrival. Oliver looked fit. "I haven't had a headache in several days. I find that very encouraging."

"It certainly is," she agreed.

A few moments later, Dr. Carter joined them carrying Oliver's records. He looked solemn as he sat down at his desk and opened the file. "There is no easy way to tell you this, Oliver. The tumor is malignant. The particular type that you have is a squamous-cell carcinoma. That is a flat, scale-like cell that, in your case, involves the epithelial tissue lining your sinus cavities. I'm not holding anything back, Oliver, because you asked me at the onset of the testing to be completely honest with you when the results were read. You have a rapidly growing carcinoma in a very dangerous location. We need to begin aggressive treatment quickly. He folded his hands on his desk and allowed Oliver and Faith a few moments to absorb everything he had said.

Faith's heart was beating so rapidly that she felt as if it were going to burst through her chest. At the same time, her mouth became dry, her palms moistened and she could feel a lump forming in her throat. She remained silent.

"How far has this progressed?" Oliver wanted to know. "I haven't had these headaches for long," he added.

"It's spreading. As I said, this type of carcinoma grows very rapidly."

"What are my options?" Oliver asked quietly.

They opted for chemotherapy, to try to shrink the tumor before going in surgically to remove it. Because of the precarious proximity to the brain, the doctor felt that if they could diminish its size before operating, it would greatly increase their margins of safety giving them a better chance of being able to remove all of the malignant tissue. The surgery, when they were ready to proceed with it, would be extensive. The team would consist of an ear, nose and throat surgeon, two neurologists and a plastic surgeon. It would be lengthy and arduous.

Faith and Oliver held great hope for this "assault," as Oliver began to refer to his treatment plan. As much as they dreaded it, they knew that they must break the news to Oliver's daughters. Once the chemo had been scheduled to begin, Oliver called Mary Jane and Brad and Jillian and asked them to come to dinner on Saturday. He asked that Mary Jane and Brad find a baby sitter for the two older boys.

"This sounds serious," Mary Jane said to her father.

"It is, my dear. Can you make it?"

"You know we'll be there, Dad."

Oliver had difficulty connecting with Jillian. He called three times and had to leave messages on her machine each time asking her to call. When he didn't hear back from her, he called a fourth time. "Jillian, this is urgent, call me!" That produced results. She told him she had spoken with Mary Jane before returning his call.

He put her on speakerphone. "So, Dad," she had said. "Why all the mystery? Aren't you even going to give us a hint? Don't tell me the marriage isn't working out."

"Jillian, I can't believe you said that. And, by the way, Faith is right here. You're on the speaker. We'll talk on Saturday. See you then, honey," he said wearily.

Though Oliver had called his daughter by an endearing name, Faith could tell by his tone that she had hurt him. She wondered what it was about Jillian that made her say such mean, spiteful things. She'd much rather be the one to put up with Jillian's ire than to have Oliver exposed to it with all he had to deal with now.

"I'll be there, Daddy. And I promise to be on time."

She hadn't apologized to him, but perhaps her promise to be on time was her way of doing so. Faith hoped she wouldn't let her father down.

Saturday Evening

Jillian was the first to arrive, but Mary Jane and Brad rang the bell less than five minutes later. Oliver mixed drinks for everyone who wanted one, and Faith brought out a couple trays of snacks.

"We can go out for dinner later, or we can order in." Once everyone had their drinks and snacks, he began. "There's no easy way to tell you this, so I'll just give you the facts. I know you've been aware of the headaches I've been having recently," he said turning to Mary Jane and Brad. "Well, I've seen an ophthalmologist recently, and he felt I needed to see my medical doctor. More to the point, I've seen an oncologist. It seems that I have a malignant tumor."

Both girls looked stunned. The color drained from Mary Jane's face. Jillian burst into tears, rose and ran into her father's arms.

CHAPTER 11

It was an unseasonably chilly afternoon in late June, when Faith and Oliver checked into the hospital the day before his surgery was scheduled. Faith spent the night wrapped in Oliver's arms.

"I love you," he whispered as she snuggled against him. "You've made me happier than I ever thought I could be again. I thank God for this time we've had together."

"Oliver, you sound as if you don't think you're going to come through this. You said the doctors have given you good odds."

Oliver was silent for a moment. "They have darling. And I'm confident I'll get well. I know I face extensive therapy afterward, but with your love and support, and our faith in God, we can beat this. I just wanted you to know how I feel about you. How very much you've given me in our short time together.

"I love you, too. You're the very best part of my life. You have to get well and you will. I don't want to go on without you, Oliver." She felt a tear escape her eye and soak into her pillow. Despite her tears, she felt relief. Oliver's hope and faith had renewed hers. She knew that together, they could face anything.

CHAPTER 12

It was a day golden with sunshine in mid-September. A soft, warm breeze gently wafted glistening grains of sand into countless irregular patterns along the deserted beach. Stately whitecaps thundered ashore only to retreat meekly to the sea with little more than a whisper. Sea oats swayed gracefully as the wind currents ebbed and flowed. Seagulls soared above, keeping a watchful eye over their watery domain.

Faith Hargrave was oblivious to the beauty that surrounded her as she pulled her white Lexus through the arched latticework beneath her ocean-front retreat in North Myrtle Beach. She was so immersed in her own sorrow that the perfection of the moment eluded her.

There had been a time, months earlier, when she would have been completely awed by the breathtaking beauty of it all. A time when she would have bounded from their car and run hand in hand with Oliver at her side to the sandy shore, laughing as she tried to keep pace with him. Kicking off her shoes at water's edge, she would have dashed into the foaming surf and waded until the water was above her knees, delighting in the moment and everything about her life. But all that seemed so long ago now, eons ago, when her world was happy, when Oliver was still with her.

For months, though she had truly tried, she had been unable to begin the healing process. Now, she had come to grieve and try to embark on the long journey toward recovery that she knew she must face. Perhaps it would be easier here, in their private retreat; in the place she felt closest to Oliver, closest to the all too brief moment in time when they had shared their lives and their dreams.

She stepped out of the car and stretched; her back felt tight and sore. Her legs were stiff. The four-hour trip down from Winston Salem, North Carolina had seemed longer than usual. And she had been tense as she drove; her head ached giving testimony to that fact.

She popped the trunk, removed her one suitcase and make-up bag and went around to the front entrance of their home. She unlocked the door and hurried to turn off the security system. One couldn't be too careful, especially after Labor Day, when so many of the houses were unattended for long periods of time. Theirs was the last house on this stretch of beachfront. She wondered if any of her immediate neighbors were here now. Perhaps she'd check later.

She walked through the spacious living room, down the hall and into their bedroom.

"Mine now," she whispered softly. "I must get used to that." She shook her head slowly, as she carried her cosmetic case into the bathroom.

She stepped over to the walk-in closet and put her suitcase down. She'd unpack later. They kept a full closet of clothes here to make traveling back and forth easier.

She turned around to Oliver's side and removed one of his sweatshirts from its hanger. As she slipped it over her head, she caught a faint scent of him, or did she just desire it so strongly that she only imagined it? She wrapped her arms tightly about herself and stood, tears welling in her eyes and spilling onto her cheeks. Perhaps this was a mistake. But, it had been no better back in Winston-Salem. No, this was right for her. She was where she needed to be; where she belonged.

She walked back through the house to the front door. She stepped out onto the broad deck that fronted the ocean. The wind whipped her clothing about her slender frame and tousled her short, blond hair, as she stood entranced, watching the magnificent whitecaps crash ashore. She stood there for some time before walking out toward the screened gazebo that marked the halfway point on the pier between the deck and the tide line where their pier ended.

She stepped inside and sank down onto a roomy, forest-green chaise lounge. She rested her head against the soft, cushioned back and closed her eyes. She remained motionless, as she willed her mind to carry her back to a happier time, to the day Oliver entered her life.

Within moments, a faint smile crossed her lips as she saw him walking toward her.

CHAPTER 13

Whenever her present became too unbearable, she allowed herself a journey into her past. Over and over, she went back to the day she had met Oliver, and the wonderful early times they shared. Her past was the only place there was any joy in her life now, and so she chose to dwell there much of the time. She always started out with those happy carefree days, but inevitably the pain of Oliver's illness crept into her thoughts, and she had to return to the present.

Faith opened her eyes. Had she been dreaming? Or only lost in her past, once again? Her cheeks were damp, there was a chill in the ocean air, and the sun was sinking into the western sky. Her heart felt heavy in her chest, she had a lump in her throat. She tried to comfort herself with the thought that she had followed both of their wishes and kept him at home during those final days.

She'd devoted all of her waking moments to keeping him as comfortable as she possibly could.

With his last breath he had whispered her name. She had felt as if her heart had been torn from her chest and yet, she couldn't will him to go on as he was for even a moment longer. She loved him far too much to see his suffering and be utterly powerless to alleviate it.

There had been some good times. They had come to the ocean retreat often, between treatments, and then for a very short time, after that long agonizing surgery. The only blessing in the surgery had been that the neuro-surgeons had been able to sever enough nerves to end the excruciating pain. They had been unable to remove the whole of the brutal tumor that ravaged her husband's brain, and ultimately imposed its toll on his entire body.

She rose from the chaise lounge, walked on down the pier and rested her arms on the rail. The water was much calmer than when she had arrived earlier in the day. In the distance she saw a large porpoise leap from the water then another, a smaller one, quickly followed suit. *Even they travel in pairs*, she reflected sadly. The ever-present sea gulls glided effortlessly above the water; a pelican swooped down and garnered his evening meal. *Yes, life goes on*, she thought to herself. *Each of us is just a tiny grain of sand at a moment in time.*

A few minutes later, Faith descended the stairs at the pier's end and stepped onto the sand. She would see if there were any signs of life at the Halls'. If she remembered right, they had planned a trip to Europe at summer's end. She wondered if they'd returned yet. She and Oliver hadn't seen much of them after Faith finished decorating the beach house. Their visits never seemed to coincide after that. In fact, they hadn't seen Oliver after he became ill. Oliver and Ben had spoken briefly on the phone once before his surgery when Ben called to plan a fishing weekend. There had been no contact after that.

When she was nearing their home, she noticed a light in one of the rooms. That didn't necessarily mean there was someone staying there. It could just mean that the timers were in good working order. She stepped onto the boardwalk that lead to their screened deck, walked between the dunes and climbed the stairs. The screen door was unlocked. She entered the large porch and rang the doorbell.

"I'll be right there." It was a woman's voice.

A moment later, the vertical blinds on the door parted and a face Faith didn't recognize peered out at her. "I'm looking for the Halls, Kitty and Ben. I'm a friend, Faith Hargrave."

The woman opened the door. "Come in. I'm Laura Hall, their daughter. I've heard them speak of you often."

"Thanks," Faith said, stepping into the kitchen area of the beach house.

"Mom's traveling with Lynette. She's thinking of writing a book set in Hawaii, and they've gone over for a few weeks, so that she can soak up some local color. Dad's working on a project in Saudi Arabia, so Mom figured she'd tag along with Lynette."

"That sounds like fun, the Hawaii part anyway. Don't think I'd be much interested in traveling to the Middle East right now."

"Is Oliver with you this trip?"

Tears welled in Faith's eyes. "No" Her voice quivered when she answered. "Oliver became ill, he had…he had surgery, but … He passed away a short time ago."

"Oh, Faith, I'm *so* sorry." Laura looked shocked. "Dad will be devastated to hear that. He had no idea that the problem was so serious. He thought so highly of Oliver. They'd been beach friends for quite some time, you know."

"Thank you." Faith managed. "Oliver was so optimistic in the beginning and he downplayed the gravity." She paused. "Well, I'd best be getting back."

Laura reached for her arm. "Come in and have a cup of tea or hot chocolate or a drink, whatever. Just come in, and keep me company. I'm here alone, and I suspect you're by yourself, too." Faith appreciated Laura's warmth and graciousness. She thought Laura looked as if she could use a little company. Perhaps it would be good for them both.

"Maybe for a few minutes. I don't need anything to drink though." She followed Laura into a sitting room. Faith noticed that Laura walked a bit slowly with a slight limp.

"I was about to mix myself a Tom Collins," Laura said, stepping over to the wet bar. "Are you sure you won't join me?"

"Okay, you've talked me into it. Besides, you shouldn't drink alone," she smiled. Faith took a seat on one of the breakfast bar stools. Laura mixed their drinks before sitting down next to her.

"I'm surprised we didn't ever see you here before. Are you not a beach lover?"

"Oh, but I am. I spent every summer here with Mom and Dad when I was a teenager. I've just been occupied elsewhere until recently."

Faith studied Laura's face as she spoke. She bore a striking resemblance to her father. She had the same round face and hazel-colored, almond-shaped eyes. She had dimples when she smiled, but her hair was dark brown and quite curly, whereas Ben's was straight and heavily sprinkled with gray. And Ben was more heavy-set than his daughter. At first glimpse, Faith would have guessed her to be near her own age, but the way she got around made her appear somewhat older.

Faith returned her attention to what Laura was saying. "A while back, I met someone on a cruise. He lived in Maryland. After several visits and a long-distance courtship, I moved to Maryland and found a job there. The relationship didn't last, but the job did. It was a pretty good one, so I stayed on. Recently, my arthritis has become so painful that Dad suggested I quit the job and move in here for a few months. It's plagued me for ten years. I have flair-ups, then it goes into remission. I guess I can thank my grandmother on Mom's side for it. Anyway, it's always been better when I'm at the shore and in a stress free environment. So, Dad 'hired' me to house-sit for them until they finish traipsing the world."

"Sounds like an ideal job to me," Faith smiled at her.

As Faith looked about the room, her eyes rested on an easel with a half-painted canvas leaning against it. It was a beautiful beginning of a seascape at twilight. "So, you're an artist," Faith said, rising and stepping closer to the canvas.

"I'm not all that good, but I love it. I find it relaxing." She smiled at Faith and flushed a bit as if she were embarrassed.

"I think that's a marvelous beginning. I can't wait to see it when it's finished. You have a fine touch and wonderful sense of color and perspective."

Faith stayed and chatted for more than an hour. Before she left, the women made arrangements to meet at nine the following morning in front of Laura's to walk along the beach to the public fishing pier. It was a mile and a half down the beach. Laura told Faith that she walked it twice daily; morning and evening. "It will be good to have the company. It's kind of lonely down here this time of year, and, since arriving, I've discovered that I'm more of a people person than I thought I was."

They walked together frequently after that. Faith found Laura very easy to talk to. She was able to speak of events connected with Oliver's death that she had told no one else. Laura listened non-judgmentally, never offering advice or condemnation at anything she told her. Faith had confided to Laura alone that she was terribly angry with God for allowing Oliver, after all he'd been through with Jane, to be stricken with cancer, to fight it so doggedly, and to suffer so terribly and ultimately to lose the battle. She felt that God had abandoned both Oliver and her when they needed him most; she was convinced He had turned a deaf ear on all of her pleas. She even confessed to Laura that she could no longer pray and that she felt desolate, defeated and utterly hollow inside much of the time.

Faith had been at the beach for several weeks, and, though she was feeling more rested than she had in months, she was still immersed in sorrow and self-pity. Suddenly her telephone rang, jarring her from her thoughts. She hurried in from the gazebo to answer it.

"Hello, stranger." It was Mary Jane. "I thought we'd hear from you. We miss you. Are you alright, Faith?"

"Yes. It's good to hear your voice, Mary Jane." Suddenly, Faith felt ashamed that she hadn't spoken with Oliver's daughter since she left Winston-Salem. Mary Jane had been wonderful through everything. She'd been supportive of Oliver and of her. And she had had a devastating loss, too.

"I have a favor to ask of you, Faith."

"Certainly. What do you need?"

"Grant has three days off from school the end of this week. Teacher work days.

He's begging me to ask you if he can come to the beach and spend that time with you."

Faith was touched. "Yes. I'd love to have him here with me for a few days. What about Christian?"

"One at a time is enough to start you out with, but thanks for asking. Anyway, play school is in session as usual. Maybe on his next break Christian can come. But there's one other thing."

"What's that?"

"Would you mind terribly coming here to get him? It's a long trip for me to make with the baby, and Brad is so tied up at work this time of year."

"That's not a problem. I have time. I can come for him."

They made the arrangements. Faith went down to tell Laura that evening. They sat on the screened deck and drank Old Fashions.

"How wonderful for you to have one of Oliver's grandsons all to yourself for a few days."

"It will be good." Faith relayed several stories of the little ones to Laura. "Oliver was crazy about those boys. I'm so pleased he got to see Taylor before…he had to leave us."

When she finished her drink, she turned to leave then stopped. "You wouldn't want to ride up with me to get Grant, would you?"

"I've improved since I arrived here but not that much. Don't think my back and legs could take that much riding right now. I'll be here when you get back. You and Grant come have supper with me Wednesday evening.

As she headed to Winston-Salem to pick Grant up, Faith found herself thinking back over the way Oliver's two daughters had reacted throughout his illness. Mary Jane had been loving and supportive, a quiet strength for Oliver and for her. She really should stay in closer touch with her; how truly thoughtless she had been. Mary Jane had tried to comfort Jillian, too. That had been a whole other chapter in the last months.

Jillian had been so needy. Faith was surprised. For a young woman who seemed so independent and was so reckless in her personal relationships, she became child-like when facing her father's eminent demise. She had made coping more difficult for Oliver. Any ground that she and Faith had made toward a truce had been lost with the announcement of Oliver's illness. It was as if she somehow blamed Faith for everything that had happened to her father. Unbelievably, the day after Oliver died, she had shown up looking for her inheritance.

"I haven't even seen your father's will, Jillian. That's been the very least of my concerns these last weeks," she had told her.

"Well, Daddy sent me money every month. He was behind when he died. You're going to have to catch that up and then continue on as Daddy would have wanted."

Faith had been sickened by her words. Oliver had loved this girl so very much. Jillian had lost a loving, caring father, and it seemed as if all she could think of was herself and how his death would affect her lifestyle.

"I'm sure you'll be well taken care of, Jillian." She felt like slapping Jillian for her hateful words and insolent tone. It was all Faith could do to keep a civil tone. Perhaps she's just in shock, she thought. Perhaps she hasn't realized all she's lost yet. She willed this to be the case for Oliver's sake even though he was not here to hear his daughter's unfeeling outburst.

"When will you check on the will? I need to know something soon. In the mean time, I'll use my credit card, but you'll have to pay it off. Daddy always did."

Two weeks after that exchange, Faith went to Oliver's lawyer's office for the reading of the will. As she approached the law offices of Whitley, Whitley, Ryan and Morgan on Country Club Road, a rather ominous feeling swept through her. What would the next hours hold for her? She desperately hoped it would be a civil gathering.

She found a parking place and went into the office. When she entered the reception area, she found Jillian already waiting there. She gave Faith a chilly nod and abruptly turned away from her. Mary Jane and Brad arrived shortly after.

CHAPTER 14

At precisely three o'clock, Aaron Whitley stepped out of his inner-sanctum and asked the Hargrave heirs to come into his private office. The client chairs were arranged in a semi-circle facing his desk. He was a man of about Oliver's age, perhaps a few years older. His short thinning hair was graying, the glasses that sat on the bridge of his nose were wire-rimmed, and he wore a navy blue, three-piece suit.

He introduced himself to those of the family he hadn't met previously and shook hands with each. "I've taken the liberty of making copies of the will for your convenience, so that you may follow along as I read through it. This is a new will. It supercedes any previous wills. It became effective April 14th of last year." He glanced at Faith. "The day of your marriage."

He removed his glasses and cleaned them with a tissue from a box on his desk then put them back on. He handed each of them a copy of Oliver's will. He sat down at his desk, and, after giving them a moment to glance over it, he began to read Oliver's last wishes aloud.

To my eldest daughter, Mary Jane Allen, her husband, Brad Allen, and their sons, Grant, Christian and their yet to be born child, I bequeath the residence they now reside in free and clear of all obligations. I leave them any and all of the furnishings that were previously mine. I leave her the Ming vase and the antique curio that belonged to her mother. I also bequeath to my daughter, Mary Jane Allen, five thousand shares of Hargrave, Taylor and Thompson common stock. Educational trusts have been established in each of their children's names with Mary Jane as the trustee.

To my daughter, Jillian Leigh Hargrave, I bequeath five thousand shares of Hargrave, Taylor and Thompson common stock. In addition, I have set up a trust to handle her education and living expenses, so long as she remains in school pursuing a career in political science or any other career choice she may desire to pursue. I hereby appoint Aaron J. Whitley, Sr., as trustee. Any proceeds left in the trust after her educational expenses have been paid, may be used by her, at the discretion of the trustee, for expenses incurred once her formal education ends and her new career begins. If any proceeds remain after such has been accomplished, they will be held in trust for her until she reaches her thirty-fifth birthday.

Jillian stiffened in her chair, noticeably shaken. Aaron Whitley read on. *To my beloved wife, Rachel Faith Inman Hargrave, I leave the house in Cayman Shores and the property at North Myrtle Beach known as Faith's Retreat. I leave her all of the remaining shares of Hargrave, Taylor and Thompson stock.*

In addition, Oliver left her shares in a variety of communication and technology stocks, three long-term CD's and a small cash savings account. He had named her as beneficiary of a modest life insurance policy he owned. His company, Hargrave, Taylor and Thompson, was the beneficiary of a large business-life policy, which had been purchased by the company.

Aaron Whitley laid the will down, took off his glasses and folded his hands on the desk. "That about does it. Of course there will be taxes to be paid, my fees, etc. It will probably take a year or more before this is all settled. Are there any questions?"

Jillian spoke up. "Why were my funds put into a trust as if I were a child? It isn't fair, and it isn't right!" she said acridly. "When did he change all this, and why?"

"Your father rewrote his will last spring, in March, to be more accurate. As I said before, it became effective on the day he and Mrs. Hargrave exchanged marriage vows."

She scowled at Faith. "You're behind this! This was all your doing!"

"Miss Hargrave, Jillian," Aaron Whitley spoke with quiet authority. "Your father told me at the time this will was written that his prospective wife had no knowledge whatsoever of what he was doing. He also wished each of his daughters to be provided for, and he set up his assets in order that this goal might be accomplished. Your funds were set in trust, as that was the way your father felt your future needs would best be served. I should think you'd be grateful."

Jillian rose. "I am grateful, but not for the way it's been set up. I'll be in touch. When can I pick up the stock certificates?"

"Those are a part of the trust that was set up," Mr. Whitley told her. "But before you leave, be sure that my secretary has a way for me to contact you. I'll need to know where to send your monthly stipend."

Jillian spun around and glared at Faith. She reached for her handbag then stormed over to the door, hair bobbing about her shoulders as she shook her head. The door banged loudly as she exited the room.

"I'm so sorry." Mary Jane looked from one to the other of those who remained. "I don't know what to say. I don't know what's gotten into Jillian. I know she adored Dad. Perhaps she's angry because he died. Everyone grieves differently. Faith, I'm especially sorry she's been so rude to you. You don't deserve it. Dad would be horrified."

"I know he would, Mary Jane. And, thank you," Faith said, fighting back tears. "I don't know what your father and I would have done without you, Brad and the boys these last months."

Aaron Whitley rose from his chair. "I have a letter for you from your husband, Mrs. Hargrave. He asked that I give it to you after the will was read." Mr. Whitley handed Faith a sealed white legal envelope.

She took it and slipped it into her purse. She would read it later, when she was alone.

Faith became aware that she was nearing Greensboro. She had barely noticed the small towns she had passed through to reach this point in the trip. She glanced at her watch. It was close to noon. She'd be at Mary Jane's in another thirty minutes or so. They'd have time for lunch and a little visit before she and Grant headed back to the beach.

When Faith and Grant arrived in North Myrtle Beach, it was after six o'clock. A brisk chilly wind whipped at their bodies as they hurried up the steps and around the deck. Faith unlocked the door. "We need to dig out some warmer clothes and a cap for you, young man. Are you still set on playing on the beach for a while today?"

"Sure. I brought two sweatshirts. I packed them myself. They both have hoods. Anyway, I like the cold."

"We'll see what we can find." Faith carried his bags into the bedroom across from hers and laid them on the bed. Grant opened the larger of them and dug out a Kelly green jacket and took a pair of high top boots out of the tote and put them on.

"Now can I go back out?"

"You may," she said giving him a little hug. She smiled. What an angelic little face stared back at her out of the hood. How glad she was to have him here with her for these few days. "But remember what I said."

"I know. Don't get farther out than my boot tops."

"No. Not even that far. Don't go further than half way up your boots. I'll be out in just a of couple minutes."

He gave her a hug. "This is great, Faith. I'm glad you let me come!"

"I am too, Grant." She walked with him to the door.

She watched him run across the deck and out to the pier. "Be careful. I'll be out with you soon," she called after him.

She unpacked Grant's bags and put his clothing in the chest of drawers in his bedroom. Then she went to her closet, took her fleece lined, emerald-green warm-up off its hanger. She stepped into the slacks, slipped her arms into the jacket and zipped it up.

She pulled a brush through her hair then wondered why she had bothered the minute she stepped out the door.

She looked around. There was no sign of Grant. She called his name. She felt panic. Where was the child? He'd been out there no more than ten minutes, if that. She had looked out once, and he'd been playing right where he'd been told to stay.

"Grant! Grant!" She cupped her hands and shouted against the wind, as she started down the beach in search of him. She had nearly reached the Halls' when she stopped and frantically called again.

A tall, sun-tanned blond man came round from the back of Laura's place. "Ma'am, are you looking for a little boy of about seven who answers to the name Grant?"

"I am. Do you know where he is?"

"Calm down. He's fine. He's out here in back with me. I'm rigging the sails on my catamaran." He turned and started around the house.

Faith caught up and kept pace with him. "Who are you? I haven't seen you around here before."

"I came in this morning and surprised Laura."

"Are you her friend from Baltimore?"

He looked down at her and laughed. "I hope she's seen the end of him. No. I'm Laura's brother, Marcus." He stopped and offered her his hand.

"I didn't know she had a brother; she hadn't mentioned you."

He laughed again. "Now, when we were kids I think she tried to forget I was around once in a while, but I thought all that was in the past."

Grant peered out at them from inside the boat as they rounded the back corner of the cottage. "Uh-oh! I'm in trouble, huh?"

"You gave me a scare young man. What should you have done?" Faith asked him.

"I know. I should have come back to the house to tell you where I was going."

"Right. And what about talking to people you don't know?"

"Don't be too rough on him," Marcus put in. "I was out on our beach, and he and I got to talking about my boat. I offered to show it to him. But she is right about talking to strangers," he said to Grant. He returned his attention to Faith. "I assume you're Faith and that you and Grant are our dinner guests tonight."

"I'm sorry. It was rude of me to ask who you were and not introduce myself. And you're right, Laura did ask us for dinner tonight. But if you and she had something planned, don't let us interfere."

"What we had planned was dinner with a very good friend of Laura's and her grandson, Grant." He looked at Faith quizzically. "You really don't look old enough to be his grandmother."

"He's my late husband's grandson. He and I were married only a short time before..." she could feel the lump forming in her throat.

"I know, Laura told me. I never met Oliver, but I heard Dad speak of him. For some reason, I thought you'd be a little older."

Laura opened the back door and stuck her head out. "Come on in before you freeze your tails off."

Dinner was delicious, and the company was very pleasant. Laura had steamed a kettle of shrimp, made hush puppies and a tossed salad. Grant loved the shrimp and hush puppies.

"Tomorrow is supposed to warm up again. What do you say to letting me take Grant out sailing?" Marcus asked after the meal.

"Cool! Is it okay, Faith? Can I go?"

"If you wear a life-jacket and promise to sit still. And if you don't go too far out," she added, looking at Marcus.

Thursday dawned sunny and much warmer than Wednesday had been. Grant gobbled down his breakfast of bacon and pancakes then announced that he was ready to go sailing with Mr. Hall.

"It's only nine-thirty, Grant. Mr. Hall said eleven o'clock."

Grant watched cartoons while Faith tidied the house and dressed for the day. At eleven, they walked the short distance to the Halls'. Marcus and two men from a shrimp boat had just finished pushing the catamaran onto the beach near the water's edge. Laura was out there, too. Grant ran to the boat.

"Good morning, small fry," Marcus greeted him. "Are you ready to set sail?"

"Yes, sir!" Grant saluted him.

"You're welcome to come along if you'd like, Faith."

"I'll take a rain check. I'll wait here with Laura."

The two women walked back to the screened deck. "How about we take a couple of these beach chairs down and watch from the beach?" Laura said reaching for a folded chair.

The breeze was gentle and mild, just enough to compensate for the warmth of the sun and keep one from becoming sticky. It was wonderfully relaxing, a perfect morning.

"Why can't everyday be like this? My back and knees feel so good. It's almost as if I don't have a thing wrong with them."

"It is gorgeous. Look out there at that ocean stretching on forever, and the sky with its billowing clouds. And just one white sail rocking gently in the waves. It looks like a painting, doesn't it?"

Laura took a camera out of her pocket and captured the scene. "You're right. I'll put that to good use later.

You seem to be happier today, Faith. I think it was a good thing for you to bring Grant down here. I think Oliver would be pleased."

"It was, and I know he would." Faith leaned her head against the back of the chair and closed her eyes. "Your brother seems nice. He's very good with Grant. But I sense that something is troubling him."

"What makes you say that?"

"Several times last evening he seemed to be somewhere else. And he looked quite sad."

"You're very observant. He is a bit troubled, but I have faith in Marcus. He'll work it all out the right way in his own time. He is good with Grant," Laura agreed pensively. "And right now, I think Grant is good for him."

"Does he have a family, children?"

"Yes…a rather large one. Oh look, they're turning around. I think perhaps they're calling it quits for today. Let's go on up to the house, and I'll see what I can find us for lunch."

Curious as Faith had become, she got the distinct impression that Laura would not be discussing her brother's situation further. And she guessed she could understand why. They might be friends. But, Marcus was blood.

CHAPTER 15

Faith found her five days with Grant nearing an end far too quickly. They took long walks on the beach and talked. She felt she was really beginning to know the child by the time Sunday arrived. They ate their breakfast in the gazebo so that Grant could say a "long good-bye" to the ocean and all its creatures.

"Can I come back soon? Please, Faith?"

"We'll see. We need to talk to your Mom and Dad about that. I know Christian wants to come too. Maybe next time, if you and your brother have a few days free together, you can both come."

"I had fun coming alone, Faith." He looked so sweet when he said it she couldn't resist pulling him to her and giving him a little squeeze.

"I know. I did, too. I liked having you all to myself."

They ate a late breakfast. Faith packed up Grant's clothes, and they were on the road by noon. Faith asked

Grant if he would like to choose some place along the way to stop and eat lunch. He was on the lookout for a Kentucky Fried Chicken within twenty minutes of embarking on the trip.

Faith stayed in Winston-Salem less than an hour, as she wanted to make it back before dark. Mary Jane tried to talk her into staying over and going back Monday morning to no avail.

"No, but thanks. I hope you understand that right now the beach house is where I need to be."

"I do. I just want you to know you're always welcome here with us."

Faith nodded and smiled as she gave Mary Jane a goodbye hug.

"Oh, I almost forgot," Mary Jane called after her. Faith stopped and turned back. "Jillian called me asking for your number at the beach. I gave it to her. I hope I did the right thing."

"That's fine. You did the right thing. I hate for you to feel that you're in the middle of this. It isn't fair to you. But we don't seem to have a choice; circumstance has put you there. Don't worry about me. I'm a big girl."

"How are things going with the Cayman Shores house? Any activity on it yet?"

"It's been shown a few times, and I've been assured that houses in Cayman Shores sell quickly. No offers yet, but it's still early. Besides, I'm told that the real estate market is rather sluggish right now."

"I'll let you go or you won't beat the sunset back. Be careful and thanks for having Grant."

"Thanks for knowing he was just what I needed."

Faith rose early Monday morning and brewed a pot of coffee. At ten o'clock, she phoned Linda Hart at her shop in Winston-Salem. Faith had tried to return to work two weeks after Oliver's funeral, but her heart wasn't in her work. She seemed to have lost all of her creativity, her drive, her motivation. She stayed on for two weeks, but it was no better by the end of that time than it had been when she first returned. She had a long talk with Linda at the close of the second week. They decided that Linda would take over for the time being, until Faith could regain her stride. Linda was extremely talented and had astute business skills. Faith had every confidence that she would run the company honestly and would probably expand their clientele more capably than she could at this time. Faith wrote letters to all of her personal clients informing them of her decision. She and Linda signed a contract between them, and Faith went into seclusion.

Shortly after, she decided to put the Cayman Shores house on the market. She told Mary Jane and Brad of her decision before listing it and they had been very supportive. She hadn't mentioned it to Jillian. She'd let Mary Jane tell her.

After it was listed, she stayed in it a short time. But once the realtors began coming through with prospective buyers, she found she couldn't stay on. It was terribly upsetting to her to think of a stranger stepping into their private world, the place that had been the catalyst in bringing Oliver into her life. Her emotions were so raw, so near the surface these days; that she seemed to be in constant emotional as well as physical pain. Throughout her entire life, she had never failed to cope with any situation that was handed her, until now. But losing Oliver had seemed to deplete her very soul. She seemed powerless over this grief that now inhabited her body and her spirit.

She suddenly became aware that Linda's answering machine had picked up, and she heard the beep to leave a message. She glanced at her watch. It was two minutes after ten. She began her message.

Linda picked up half way through. "I just walked in, and my hands were full. I'm glad I caught you before you hung up."

"How are you?"

"I'm fine, and business is great. In fact, I had planned to call you later today. I think we need to hire another associate if you aren't ready to come back yet. At the very least, we need someone part time."

By the time their conversation ended, they were in agreement. Linda would hire a young mother, Diana Clifton, whom she had met recently. Diana had a degree in design from State and wanted to return to a work schedule of twenty to twenty-five hours a week. Linda liked her, and Faith thought it sounded workable.

Faith busied herself puttering about the house for the next hour. When the phone rang, she braced herself in anticipation of Jillian's call. She knew that if Jillian had asked Mary Jane for her number, it would only be a matter of time before she'd hear from her. It was a wrong number.

After having had Grant's company for several days, she found the house lonely. She walked down to visit with Laura in the early afternoon but found no one at the house. She walked along the beach. She found a perfect sand dollar, rinsed it clean and took it home with her.

After dinner she curled up on the sofa, draped a soft angora blanket over her legs and began to read. A few minutes later the phone rang, and she reached for the receiver.

"Hello."

"Hello, Faith. It's Jillian." She sounded civil enough. "So, how are you these days?"

"I'm doing okay, thanks. How about you?"

"I've been better. I've run into a little problem. I need some money."

"What kind of problem? How much do you need?

"It's kind of personal. I need seventy-five-hundred."

"Jillian, I don't have that kind of money to give you, right now. I'm..."

"That's crap! Dad left you loaded. Two houses, stocks, and...no trustee for you to answer to."

"Have you talked to Mr. Whitley about this?" She tried to control her growing anger toward the girl.
"I have. He won't let me have it. Says he can't. He treats me like a child! Can you believe he's put me on 'an allowance' as he calls it now?"

"He's only following..."

Jillian cut in. "Damn! It's my money! I should be able to get it when I need it. Can't you let me have it, even as a loan?"

"You have a mistaken idea of your father's assets. There were a lot of bills at the end. The reason I'm selling the Cayman Shores house is because I have to. The estate hasn't even been settled yet."

"I knew you were going to be difficult. You say you want to be my friend. Well, you don't care about me, and you don't care what happens to me. You're all wrapped up in yourself! I don't know what Dad *ever* saw in you."

Instantly, tears stung Faith's eyes. "I'm sorry you feel that way, Jillian," she managed to say. "I'm going to hang up now."

Afterward, she buried her face in a sofa pillow and dissolved into tears.

She wanted so to make peace with Oliver's youngest daughter. But buying it wouldn't be the answer, even if she had the funds. The girl needed to grow up; she'd been spoiled and coddled enough. Faith understood that Jillian was angry because she had told her no. Still, Jillian's words had hurt her deeply. Could anything ever bring them together?

Faith rose and walked into the bedroom and over to the dresser. She pulled the top drawer open and removed the envelope that Aaron Whitley had given her in his office after the will had been read. She opened it and removed the stationary inside. She had read Oliver's letter often. She could almost recite it from memory. But it was always comforting to her to remove the paper that he had touched, press it to her lips and read the words that he had meant for her alone. And so she unfolded the treasured stationary once again.

CHAPTER 16

Faith darling,

I have instructed Aaron Whitley to see that you receive this letter after the reading of my will. It is meant for your eyes alone. I want you to know how very much you have enriched my life, though we had far too little time together. In the brief period we did have, you made me feel whole again, complete. Loving you was the best part of every hour of every day for me.

Your tenderness and devotion gave me both joy and sorrow as the inevitable approached. Joy, from your warm, loving, ever-constant presence throughout my illness. Sorrow, because I knew the hour was at hand when I would have to leave you.

In my will, I have tried to provide for those who were dearest to me. I have given to my daughter Mary Jane that which I thought she would most treasure, the home where she grew up with all its happy memories. And I have left her shares of stock in the company that I helped establish. I am so proud of the woman she has become. I love her dearly. Her thoughtful ways and fierce loyalty remind me so much of her mother. She and her wonderful family have been a source of strength for me and I know, for you, also. I am eternally grateful to them and have conveyed these feelings to them.

I have also tried to provide for my daughter Jillian in the way that she will best be served by her inheritance. This may come as a surprise to you, but I have been aware for quite some time that she harbors hostile, resentful feelings toward you, even though she has tried to hide it from me. And I know that you are aware of this but would never mention it.

As I have told you, I bear some of the responsibility for the fact that she has grown into a spoiled, self-centered young woman. I wish I could change that for Jillian's sake, but I cannot. For this reason, I have taken away any and all of your need to have authority over her financial affairs by appointing my friend and attorney, Aaron Whitley, as the trustee of all of her funds, including the shares of stock which I have left her. It is my fervent wish that in doing so; I remove a great obstacle from you and perhaps open the door to a better relationship between the two of you in the future. I feel she would benefit from becoming closer to you. I know you are eager to embrace her friendship, if she will only give you the opportunity.

To you, my darling, I've left the bulk of my estate. I'm sorry that I haven't more to give. I have had some financial reverses in the last several years. Therefore, I've been unable to leave the Cayman Shores and Faith's Retreat properties free and clear. Though I put significant cash into each of them, both still carry relatively large mortgages. Perhaps if you sell one, it will free up considerable equity to invest in the other. I leave up to you as to how you wish to handle that matter. Many of my investments are at market lows at this time. Hopefully they will rebound in the future.

Finally, my love, I know this is not the future we had envisioned, but I hope that you will go on for both of us. You're young, beautiful and talented. You have gifts to give and to receive. Don't live in the past, my darling. Embrace the future for both of us.
My eternal love,
Oliver

"Oh, Oliver, I'm really trying," she whispered against the pages. "Nothing has ever been so difficult, but I'm trying." Tears blurred her vision as she folded the letter, placed it in its envelope and returned it to the drawer.

The next couple of days were uneventful. She truly expected that Jillian would call again, but she hadn't. Wednesday evening she had gone into the kitchen to check the pantry and decide what to eat for dinner when the phone rang. She braced herself and lifted the receiver.

"Hello," she said so firmly that she even surprised herself.

"Faith! What's wrong? You don't sound like yourself."

It was Laura. She felt her spirits lift. "Oh, I'm sorry. I was expecting someone else. How are you?"

"Glad I wasn't that someone else, I think!" She laughed. "I called to see if you'd come have dinner with Marcus and me. We've just returned from visiting with an aunt and uncle in Wilmington."

"Thanks. Dinner sounds nice. I wondered where you were. I've missed you and was concerned that maybe your arthritis had acted up."

"I should have told you, but we just decided to drive up on the spur of the moment and you weren't back yet. My arthritis has been better, but it's also been a whole lot worse. Marcus didn't want to leave before talking with our Uncle Charles. I think he'll be going back tomorrow. If not then, the next day for sure."

"What time would you like to have me come?"

"Anytime you want to. I was about to mix us an old fashioned."

"See you soon. Thanks again." Faith hung the receiver up.

She felt safer knowing that Laura was back at the cottage again. Faith had become quite fond of her. There was such an easy, quiet countenance about Laura. Faith was completely at ease with her, a fact she found remarkable, given that they had known one another for only a few weeks. She sensed that Laura carried an inner burden, that she had been terribly hurt; perhaps by the man from Baltimore. She had been rather flip in telling about the breakup that first day when they had met, but Faith suspected that the wound was still raw. Laura never complained, though, about anything. Not even on several occasions when Faith could tell she was in a great deal of pain. Laura was absolutely not one to indulge in self-pity.

And she was trustworthy. Faith felt she could talk to her about anything, and it would remain a confidence between them. Just as she didn't discuss her brother's affairs, Faith knew that what she said to Laura was just between them, too. She thought that a rare quality in a woman. She, too, strove for that attribute. It had been difficult when it came to Jillian's treatment of her, but she had remained true to her principles.

Faith went into her bathroom and sat down at the vanity. She brushed her hair, put lipstick on for the first time that day and dabbed a little blusher on her cheeks. She had gained such a tan, that even though it was the fall of the year she didn't need much make-up. She brushed a bit of mascara onto her lashes and left.

When she reached the Halls', Laura and Marcus were sitting on the screened deck. They appeared to be engaged in a serious discussion. Faith coughed to announce her arrival as she started up the steps.

Marcus rose promptly, walked to the screen door and held it open for her. "There she is!" He grinned at her. "Come on in, have a seat." He motioned her toward the glider. "Shall I pour you an old fashioned?"

"Yes. That sounds good, thank you."

Laura rose. "I'll get it. I need to check on dinner anyway. I'm trying out a new chicken dish. My Aunt Jean gave me the recipe yesterday before we left. It sounded so good that I thought I'd make you two my guinea pigs."

Faith noticed that she rose with a little more difficulty than usual. When she disappeared into the house, Faith turned her attention to Marcus. "Laura tells me you'll be leaving soon."

"Yes. The way it looks now, I'll probably go Friday. I need to be back by the weekend." He looked quite solemn, almost as if it would be painful to leave.

"You love the ocean, don't you?"

"That I do. It's been in my blood since I was a kid, about Grant's age as a matter of fact. Dad bought the place when I was seven, Laura had just turned eleven, and she always referred to it as the best birthday present she ever got. Dad never told her any differently."

"She hasn't told me that it's hers yet," Faith laughed. "Do you get down here often?"

"No. Not nearly enough, especially in the last several years. I miss it. It's the one place I've always been able to clear my head, do my best thinking. Make my most important decisions." He looked pensive, far away.

As she sat watching him, Faith got the distinct feeling that he was no longer aware of her presence sitting on the glider across from him. She couldn't help wondering what it was that he was having such a difficult time resolving.

Laura rejoined them. "Dinner's almost ready. It looks great, if I do say so myself. Hope it tastes as good as it looks. You might as well come on in now."

"It sure smells good. I got a whiff of it when you opened the door," Marcus said, rising from his chair.

They were just finishing the meal when the phone rang. "I'll get it," Laura said reaching for the portable receiver. "Oh, Dad! What a nice surprise! How is the world traveler?" She listened. "Is Mom back yet?" A pause. "That sounds like fun for her." Another pause. "Yes." She began stacking their dirty dishes in front of her as she listened to her father. "Marcus is here; he came last week. We visited Aunt Jean and Uncle Charles for a couple days and just got back." A pause. "No. Would you like to talk to him?"

Abruptly, she rose and left the room. Marcus's eyes followed his sister. He sighed and shook his head. "Excuse me, Faith." He rose hastily, walked to the back door and stepped outside letting the door bang shut.

Suddenly, Faith felt like a fifth wheel. She wasn't sure what to do. She didn't want to walk through the den to get to the deck, and she certainly didn't want to go out back. She couldn't help hearing some of Laura's end of the conversation.

"Dad, I think that's unreasonable." Silence. "Some things take time. But Dad…" A pause. "And that's exactly why we went to see Uncle Charles. But…"

Faith rose from the table and began gathering the dishes and carrying them to the sink. She turned the water on and began rinsing the dirty dishes, but she could still hear Laura.

"No one can make someone else's life choices for them." Pause. "I know that. But you don't walk in his shoes, either." After a moment, "Dad, I don't want to discuss this any further. Give Mom my love when she gets home. I love you, Dad. Bye." She stayed in the den for a moment longer before she returned to the kitchen.

"Thanks for doing the dishes. That was nice of you."

"I should really be going. Thanks for a delicious dinner, Laura. You're welcome to try out all your new recipes on me."

Laura gave her a hug. "Thanks, Faith. I'll talk to you tomorrow. Let's walk in the morning."

"A morning walk sounds good."

"I'll be ready whenever you get here."

Faith left through the front door to avoid intruding on Marcus's privacy. When she reached her place, she decided to walk a little farther down the beach before going in.

The moon looked like an artist's painting tonight. It was gorgeous, nearly full, with billowing-translucent clouds drifting across it. A few minutes later she saw a man walking toward her. As he drew a little closer, her pulse quickened. He looked like Oliver, and for a split second her impulse was to run to him. But she didn't. She stood perfectly still. The man waved at her. She watched him, transfixed. As he drew closer, she recognized Marcus. She hadn't realized how similarly he and Oliver were built. They were the same height with broad shoulders, trim waist and long legs. The shape of their heads and hairstyle, even Marcus's blond hair looked silver, here in the moonlight, as this silhouette of a man continued on toward her. She felt unnerved. She began to tremble.

He reached her. He could see that she was shaken. "I didn't mean to frighten you," he said, putting his hand on her shoulder. "Come on. I'll walk you back to your place. You don't need to be out here alone in the dark."

He released her shoulder. They walked to her home. Neither of them spoke.

CHAPTER 17

Faith dreamed of Oliver throughout most of that night. When she awakened the next morning she didn't feel rested. She lay in bed a while longer hoping to go back to sleep, but she couldn't. She finally gave up, rose and dressed for her walk on the beach with Laura. When she stepped outside she found the air much chillier than she was expecting. *Must have had a cold front come through,* she thought. She went back in and grabbed her red fleece hooded windbreaker.

It was after ten when she reached Laura's front door. She knocked. After a moment, Laura opened the door. One look at her friend told Faith that Laura was in pain. Laura stepped out onto the porch and shivered. Her gait was slow and her movements stiff.

"Do you want to skip the walk today and just stay here and visit?"

"No. I need to keep moving. Let me grab a coat with a hood and some gloves, and I'll be right with you."

Poor Laura, she thought to herself. It must be awful to be so young and have such a problem. Sadly, she knew her friend's condition would only worsen as she grew older.

They walked only a quarter of the way to the pier today, but it took as long as when they walked all the way on one of Laura's good days. When they reached Laura's cottage on their return, she invited Faith in.

"No. I have some things I need to do today. I made a promise to myself that I'd start looking for some place to rent a little office space. Maybe I'll contact some realtors and introduce myself; see if we might make a referral arrangement. I need to start working again. I think I need to try to sell the business in Winston-Salem though. I may call Linda and see if we can work out an arrangement."

"Good for you, girl!"

"I'll see you later." Faith headed on down the beach.

"Oh! I almost forgot," Laura called after her.

Faith stopped and turned back to her friend.

"If I'm not better by tomorrow, would you mind driving Marcus to the airport?"

"I'll be glad to. Let me know in the morning. What time does he leave?"

"I think it's three o'clock, but I'll check with him. We'll let you know for sure.

Laura's arthritis was worse on Friday. Marcus called Faith at nine to say that he was taking his sister to get a cortisone injection.

"I'm so sorry. Let me know when you get back."

"Will do. I guess I'll need to impose on you to get me to the airport this afternoon."

"It's no imposition. I'm happy to feel useful. What time do you think we need to leave?"

Take-off time is 4:07. So, I guess we should leave here no later than two-thirty. It's a pretty good drive."

Faith fixed herself a grilled cheese sandwich for lunch and was eating when her phone rang. "Now who?" she asked aloud.

"Hello."

"Faith?"

"Yes."

"This is Barbara Fields.

"Yes, Barbara. How are you?" Barbara was the real estate agent with whom she had listed the Winston-Salem house.

"I'm well, thank you. I have an offer on your house. It isn't what you were hoping for, but I have to present it. And," she added, "we can always counter."

The figure Barbara quoted her was very disappointing. "Let me think about it. I'll definitely counter if I don't just turn it down flatly. I can't afford to accept that figure.

When Faith arrived at the Halls' at two-thirty, Laura was in bed. Marcus carried his suitcase out and put it in Faith's trunk.

"Why don't you drive if you know the way," Faith said, handing him the keys.

Forty-five minutes later they saw a sign that the airport was three miles ahead. It began to rain. "Here comes the rest of that front," Marcus said, as he turned on the windshield wipers.

The rain grew heavier as they drove on. By the time they reached the airport, Marcus had slowed to twenty-five miles an hour just to see. The sky was nearly black.

He checked his watch. There was still over half an hour before the plane was scheduled to take off. "It looks like the rain is here to stay for a while. I wouldn't try to drive until it lets up some. Come on in with me, and, after I get checked in, I'll buy us a cup of coffee."

The line was short at baggage check. They found a coffee shop and sat down at one of the tables. "Would you like anything besides coffee?"

"No thanks. And, I think I'd rather have a coke."

Marcus went over to the counter and brought back two cokes. "I feel much better leaving Laura today knowing that you're just a few houses down the beach from her."

"Do you think I should stay down there tonight? I hate to think of her all alone in the condition she's in."

"It might not be a bad idea. Laura thinks you're special. I'm glad you became friends. She needs you right now."

"I need her, too." Faith was surprised to hear herself admit it.

An announcement came over the loudspeaker. "Passengers for U.S. Airways flight 7926 for Philadelphia, may I have your attention please. Your flight has been delayed due to weather conditions. The new time of departure is 5:45. Thank you."

"That's me." Marcus shrugged his broad shoulders, sighed and looked resigned. They finished their cokes then walked out into the waiting area so Faith could check on the weather. It was still pouring, flashes of lightning illuminated the sky every few seconds and the wind gusts had reached squall intensity.

"I guess you'll have company while you wait," she told him. "At least for a while."

"Good."

He seemed in better spirits today than he had been when he told her he was leaving; noticeably better than when he left the house abruptly after dinner Wednesday evening, and later that same evening when he had remained silent as he walked back with her to her beach house.

As if he had read her mind, he turned to her. "I should apologize for leaving the table so abruptly. I'm at...." He stopped.

"I understand, believe me. I didn't take it personally."

"I've come to a crossroad in my life right now." He began again, "My father doesn't understand. There are things he doesn't know. Feelings are very strained between us. I hate it. We've had a close relationship in the past." He looked pensive again.

"I'm at a crossroad, too. I've been there for months. I just can't seem to move beyond it. I went home yesterday to make some phone calls, and I didn't do it. I found a dozen excuses to put them off, until it was too late in the day to make them. I've never been through anything in my life that was as difficult as these last ten months have been. I've never faced a situation that I was unable to cope with until this happened to me. I can appreciate what you must be going through even though I don't know what it is. And, no one else can tell you how to deal with it. You absolutely have to do it in your own way."

"Thank you, Faith," he said quietly. He reached for her hand and gave it a little squeeze before releasing it.

The rain had turned back to drizzle. "I guess I'd better head back toward home before it starts up again."

"Good idea. Tell Laura I'll call her after I get back tonight. Thanks for the ride and the company."

As she drove back, she reflected on her conversation with Marcus. She found him as easy to talk to as Laura. Perhaps it ran in the family. Still, he and his father were definitely at odds. From what she had overheard Wednesday night, it sounded as if his father had refused to speak with him. Then Marcus had looked upset as he left the house. What could be so awful that you would lose a parent's ear? When she had mentioned to Laura that she thought he was good with Grant and had asked if he had a family, Laura had said he had a large one. And, she said that Grant was good for him, too. Were he and his wife having problems? Perhaps trying to decide whether to separate or not? And, what about the children? Marcus had said his father didn't understand.

Perhaps the blame wasn't all one sided. Perhaps there were things that he was keeping in confidence to shield someone. All Faith knew was that she found him to be a very kind man, and he certainly seemed to be a devoted brother. As she drove on, Faith realized that her mood was better for the time she'd spent with Marcus.

Faith spent the night at the Halls' beach house. Laura insisted that she was feeling much better after the injection and her day of rest, but Faith stayed anyway. When Marcus called it was after midnight. Laura answered the phone and they spoke for several minutes. She relayed to Faith that his plane had been further delayed from take-off by bad weather on the other end and he had just walked in the door.

Laura was much improved the next morning, and Faith returned to her own place after she fixed their breakfast. She had been contemplating the offer on her house in Winston-Salem all morning. She had decided to turn the offer down. She felt it was too low to even waste her time countering. Surely something better would come along. She started in to her bedroom to get Barbara Fields' business card out of her dresser drawer, but her phone rang before she reached the bedroom. She answered.

"Hello, Rachel."

It sounded funny. She hadn't been called Rachel since before she'd married Oliver, except by Linda Hart. "Yes. Fran Thompson? Is that you?"

"Yes. Faith," she corrected herself. "How are you? I've missed you. I called Mary Jane to get your number. I hope that was okay."

"That's fine. I'm doing," she hesitated, "well. Better than I was anyway."

"Good. Listen, Faith. I have some very disturbing news. I hate to have to be the one to call you with this, but Henry and I felt that you needed to know before Monday. We wanted to warn you. So you could protect yourself."

CHAPTER 18

Faith was stunned. "Protect myself? From what?"

"*The Journal* is going to break the story Monday. Two of the associates at Hargrave, Taylor and Thompson are going to be charged with embezzlement. You do remember that I told you some time back about internal problems, don't you?"

"Yes. But I had no idea it was anything like that! I thought it was falling stock prices, personality clashes or power struggles, all of which are bad enough."

"Well, it's big! They're talking nearly a million over a matter of months."

"Do you know who they are, Fran?"

"Don't let it out until it breaks in the papers, but yes. The treasurer, John Merrill and Scott Hansen, one of the junior partners."

"Oh, my gosh! I find that hard to believe. How awful!"

"That's not the worst part, Faith. I hate to be the one to tell you this, but the scuttlebutt is, they're implicating Oliver! They're saying that he was behind the whole scheme."

Faith was speechless. An involuntary shudder shook her as a chill shot through her body. She felt as if she had run head-on into a twenty-ton iceberg. She sank onto the bed feeling sick.

"Faith? Are you still with me? Did you hear what I just said?"

"Yes," she replied finding her voice. "Surely no one believes them. You don't, do you?"

The line was silent for a moment.

"Well, do you, Fran?"

"Of course not. Why do you think I'm calling you? Henry doesn't either. He thought you should hear it from a friend before the story breaks. We wanted to warn you, because you know it's going to be all over TV as well as in all of the area papers. We thought you'd want to talk to the girls before Monday."

"Yes, of course. Thanks, Fran, you're a good friend. I do need to talk with them. You didn't mention anything to Mary Jane, did you?"

"No. Not a word. I thought it should come from you."

"Oh, Fran, I can't believe they'd try to implicate Oliver. He was a founder of the company. Why would anyone think he would do something so terrible to his own company?"

"I agree with you, Faith. And we're going to work to clear his name. Hargrave, Taylor and Thompson hired a law firm on Friday. But there's more."

Oh, God, spare me! Faith wanted to scream. But, she remained silent.

"You know how dismal the last quarter earnings were. That, coupled with the scandal that will break on Monday, is going to cause the stock to take an even further nosedive. It's already at a three-year-low. Henry says that you and the girls ought to contact your broker first thing Monday morning and sell off all of your shares. He knows you've had some pretty heavy expenses lately and hates to see you lose the money that's invested in your stock on top of everything else."

"My mind is churning right now, Fran. I do appreciate your warning. I have so much to think about, to sort out. I'll be back in touch with you. You two have been great throughout Oliver's illness and now this. Please thank Henry for me." They said goodbye.

Faith felt absolutely crushed. The heaviness in her chest and stomach had the sensation of a vice cutting off her ability to breathe. She had thought that nothing could be worse than losing Oliver. Not only had she lost this wonderful man; now those dreadful men, at the company that he founded, were trying to tarnish his good name in an attempt to save their own hides. She forced herself to inhale slowly and deeply.

"Think! Think, girl," she said aloud. "You have to do something!" Her words seemed to reverberate about the room. "Think!" she commanded again. But her mind was anesthetized for the moment.

CHAPTER 19

It was a full thirty minutes before Faith pulled herself together enough to call Mary Jane. She tried not to let her voice reveal her inner turmoil when Oliver's daughter answered. "I'd like to drive up to Winston-Salem this afternoon and stay over with you if that's okay. I may need to be there for several days."

"Wonderful! We'd love it. The boys will be so excited. I was going to call you this evening just to visit. This will be much better."

How comforting it felt to hear Mary Jane's voice and to feel so welcomed by her. "I'll throw a few things into a suitcase when we hang up and be on my way."

"Sounds great! Drive carefully."

"Oh, I almost forgot to ask. Would you mind calling Jillian and asking her to come to town tomorrow afternoon?"

"Sure, I will." Mary Jane sounded puzzled.

I'd like to talk to her, too. I think she'd be more receptive to your request than mine."

"Consider it done, Faith. I hope she hasn't been hassling you. I was a little concerned when I gave her your phone number. Sometimes Jillian can act like a twenty-one-year-old going on six or seven.

"She did call. But, only once." Faith didn't want to get into their discussion with Mary Jane, though she surmised that Mary Jane had a pretty good idea of what Jillian wanted from her. "I'll see you later today."

When Faith finished packing, she phoned Laura. "Something has come up. I need to make an unexpected trip to Winston-Salem. I'll probably be gone for several days. I'll tell you about it when I get back. If you need to reach me, this is Mary Jane and Brad's number."

"Thanks. I hope there isn't a problem."

Faith didn't respond to Laura's concern. "I hate to have to run off when you aren't feeling well. I'll be back as soon as I can."

"Don't give it a second thought. I'll be fine. I'm getting around even better now than I was this morning."

"I'll call to check on you."

"Thanks. Now go on, and have a good time. And, be careful."

Faith locked the house, put her luggage in the trunk and headed out of town. Twenty miles into the trip, she felt her nerves beginning to ease slightly. She was doing something. She was taking action. This was good. It had just taken her a little while to fully comprehend and then begin to deal with Fran's disclosure. Now the initial shock she felt was replaced by anger. The accusations of Oliver's part in it seemed absolutely incredible to her.

I won't let them implicate you when you aren't here to defend yourself. I'll do everything in my power to prevent them from dragging your name through the mud, Oliver.

She looked down at the speedometer. It was inching toward seventy-five as she sped on down the two lane country road. Almost too late, she saw the tractor pull out onto the highway in front of her and oncoming traffic in the lane to her left. She gasped as she slammed on her brakes. Her wheels screeched as the car veered left. She pumped the brakes and veered back to the right before she was able to stop just inches behind the tractor.

"Thank you, Lord," had been the first words out of her mouth.

Her car sat motionless in the middle of the road. She was trembling. The farmer hollered an obscenity at her and drove on. She continued to sit there while she tried to calm herself. The driver in the car behind her honked and gave her a hand gesture. She waved him around her. She took a deep breath. Only then, did she realize what she had said. She had given a little prayer of thanks. She had spoken to God for the first time in months. He had been there for her. Instinctively, she had given him credit for her escape from disaster.

She shook her head. "No! No," she said. "You don't get off that easily. I'm still too angry with You. You stole the joy from my life. I'm the one who put the brakes on. I saved me, not You."

She continued on toward Winston-Salem, taking care to concentrate on her driving and obey the speed limit for the remainder of the trip. It was late afternoon when she reached Mary Jane and Brad's.

They had dinner and spent a pleasant evening together until it was time for the boys to go to bed. Brad was watching TV in the den, when Mary Jane and Faith came back downstairs after tucking the three little ones in,

"I need to talk to you both about a very serious matter," Faith began.

They looked at her in surprise. Mary Jane picked up the remote and turned the TV off. "What is it? Is it Jillian?"

"No. It concerns the company, Hargrave, Taylor and Thompson, and much more." She had their full attention. She relayed the details of her phone conversation with Fran Thompson.

"Oh, dear God! I don't believe for one minute that my father would ever be involved in anything like that. I'm shocked and hurt that anyone at that company would accuse him."

"It's inconceivable!" Brad said. He rose and walked over to the desk and opened the drawer. He removed a spiral notebook, returned to the sofa and began to make notes as Faith continued talking. When she finished with everything Fran had said the women sat silently waiting for Brad to finish.

After a few minutes, he stuck his pen behind his ear.

"I like to get things in black and white; it helps me think better. This is the way I see the situation. John Merrill, the treasurer of the company and Scott Hansen, a junior partner are about to be charged with embezzlement. Henry Thompson, for whatever reason, asked his wife to forewarn you about something that they expect to happen on Monday. They suggest that you unload your stock first thing Monday, hopefully before the story breaks. While his intentions may be the very best, that warning falls under the category of insider trading. If anyone in the company goes out and dumps their stock before the general public gets wind of the scandal, that's illegal."

"They've been great support for me throughout the past months. I'd hate to see them get into problems for trying to help me now. That would make this entire situation all the more troubling.

"I agree. They have been."

"You, Mary Jane, Jillian and I, together, control fifty one percent of the outstanding stock in the company," Faith said.

"That's right. We do," Brad said.

"Suppose we hang on to it," Mary Jane joined in.

"Exactly," Faith said. "We maintain control of the voting rights if we stick together even if the stock price does drop significantly."

"Jillian's going to give us problems, I know my sister. She's looking for money for something; I'm not sure what. She's called me about it recently, and I'll bet that's what she called you about, too."

"Yes. But you forget. Her shares are in trust so it's really up to Aaron Whitley."

"That's right," Brad added. "Did Fran Thompson mention anything about a board meeting?"

"No. Not to me. But we'll certainly need one. They'll need to fill the treasurer's position right away, too. And, they need to address damage control."

"If no one else does, then Faith, you need to call for an emergency meeting just as soon as possible," Brad said. He rose and began to pace.

"You're right," Faith agreed.

"As to your thoughts on holding your stock, you're right about that, too. This is no time to panic," Brad continued. "If a large number of the securities are dumped in the light of all this scandal, the stock price will fall out of bed. We need to keep our wits about us, think clearly along every avenue of this." He paused as the phone rang. "I'll get it." Brad lifted the receiver to his ear.

"Hello." A silence. "Yes. Hello, Henry." A pause. "Yes. She is. She arrived this afternoon. Decided she'd come to town in light of all the happenings." Another silence. "We were discussing their options when you called." A long silence ensued. "I'll pass that on to Faith and the girls. Thanks for your concern. One more thing, Henry. Has anyone called for a board meeting yet?" Brad nodded as he listened. "Good. It's definitely called for. There is a great deal that needs to be resolved. Keep us informed. Thanks." He hung the receiver up.

"Henry and Steven Taylor are trying to reach the board members now to set a time. They don't think there should be a problem meeting the two-thirds quorum. He'll be back to us with a day and time. He and Steven are aiming for late Monday afternoon.

"Did you reach Jillian? Is she coming?"

"I did," Mary Jane said. "And, she said she'd try. I guess I didn't press her about it as hard as I should have."

"Now that we know the gravity of all of this, I'll get her down here," Brad said, reaching for the receiver.

While Brad spoke with Jillian, Faith went into the study and used her cell phone to call Aaron Whitley.

"Mr. Whitley, I'm sorry to bother you this late, and at home. But we need to speak with you urgently. Is there any way you could come to Mary Jane and Brad's house tonight? Or, if you'd rather meet at your office, we'll come there."

"Can you tell me what this concerns? I'm not feeling very well tonight."

"It concerns Oliver's company." She still thought of Hargrave, Taylor and Thompson as his, even though he'd been gone for months. "It concerns a scandal that's about to break and the company stock."

There was a pause on Aaron's end of the line. "I know you wouldn't call me if you didn't feel it was urgent. Give me thirty minutes. I'll meet you at my office."

"Thanks. We'll be there." They hung up. Faith rejoined Mary Jane and Brad in the den.

Brad had reached Jillian on her cell phone. "She says she'll be here by two tomorrow afternoon."

"Mr. Whitley agreed to meet us at his office in half an hour."

"You and Brad go," Mary Jane offered. "I'll stay here with the boys."

When they reached Aaron Whitley's office, Faith and Brad had to wait in the parking lot for ten minutes before he drove up. Once inside, they followed Mr. Whitley into the conference room. All three sat at one end of the massive oak table.

"Now, what's this all about young lady?" Aaron asked in a gravelly voice.

He blew his nose. "Sorry to bring you out at this hour. But, as I told you on the phone, I'm a bit under the weather and my office is a halfway point between our two homes."

Faith quickly went through the story trying not to leave anything out. She told him what she, Brad, and Mary Jane had discussed about holding the stock through all of this. She saved the accusations against Oliver until last.

Aaron Whitley rose from his chair shaking his head. He stepped over to the water cooler and filled a paper cup for himself. "That's incredible. There is no way Oliver would be involved. I've known him for nearly twenty years. What evidence do they have? Just the word of two accused embezzlers?"

"I don't know," Faith answered. "I was so stunned by Fran Thompson's call that I didn't ask much of anything. But, that's a very good question, isn't it?"

"Yes it is." Aaron looked at Brad. "And, you're absolutely right about the insider trading. That could end up being added to the list of the company scandals, if Henry Thompson doesn't get his act straightened out. His desire to help you would only add to the problem that apparently already exists. Someone needs to talk to him; set him straight."

Brad nodded. "You're right. Also, I've spoken with Jillian. She'll be here tomorrow afternoon."

Aaron smiled as he returned to his seat. "Miss Jillian Hargrave," he said. "She'll really be putting the pressure on me to sell her stock now. She's quite upset with me these days, because she can't twist me around her little finger like she could her father. In all the years I knew Oliver, I'd have to say that daughter Jillian was his one weakness.

Just couldn't seem to say 'no' to that girl. But why did you call Jillian? She doesn't have any say in this. I'm the trustee. I make the decisions for her."

"We thought we needed to break the news about the accusations against her father before she read it in the paper or heard it on TV," Faith replied.

"Yes. You do have a point there," Aaron agreed. "You're on the Board of Directors now, aren't you, Faith?"

"Yes. I am. I was voted on when they lost Oliver."

"Have they scheduled a meeting to deal with this yet?"

"Henry Thompson and Steven Taylor are working on that now."

"Hmm." Aaron looked pensive. He sat quietly for a moment. Finally, he picked up a pen and began to write. "I'm going to give you a list of questions that you need to make sure you get answered at that meeting."

CHAPTER 20

At 2:00 a.m. Sunday, Faith, Mary Jane and Brad sat around the kitchen table, drinking decaf and discussing options.

"You know," Brad began, "I'm inclined to think it might not be a bad idea to ask Aaron Whitley to accompany you to that board meeting. And, he has every right to be there as the trustee of Jillian's estate. I think you'll benefit from having a legal perspective of that meeting. Everyone else is concerned about the company and their jobs. You have an added concern. Oliver; and what someone is trying to do to him."

"That's a good point, Brad. I'll call him in the morning." Faith leaned back in her chair and yawned. "I don't know about you two, but I'm beat. I have to get some sleep." She glanced over at Mary Jane and saw that her lids were drooping. "It looks like I'm not the only one." "We could all use some shut-eye," Brad said, pushing his chair back from the table.

Sunday morning, Faith called Aaron Whitley trying to catch him before he left for church. She left a message asking him to return her call in the afternoon. Jillian arrived at a little after two o'clock.

"So, what's all the mystery? Brad, you were so secretive on the phone last night."

Weighing her words carefully, Mary Jane relayed the events of the last twenty-four hours to her sister. The emphasis was basically on their father's involvement. They had agreed the night before that the less threat Jillian felt to her financial welfare, the more cooperative she'd be. Though they down-played it, they knew she was a bright girl; she'd figure it out for herself once she became reconciled in her own mind as to what was happening to her late father.

"Jeez. I'm not believing this!" She slouched back more deeply into the cushy forest green and burgundy plaid sofa. "How could anyone say that about Dad?"

"When a man's desperate, he'll do about anything to save his own hide. What better scapegoat do they have than a man who can no longer defend himself?" Faith said quietly.

Jillian gave her a cool look. "Jeez, how's that gonna affect me in Chapel Hill? Do you think it'll make the papers there? And, I already owe a ton of money. That prick Aaron Whitley won't give me a dime over my 'allowance.' Shit!"

"Damn it, Jillian! Are you all you ever think of? What's wrong with you?" Mary Jane jumped to her feet. She looked close to tears. "I can't believe you. Listen to yourself. Think about Dad or someone besides yourself and how everything is going to affect you for once in your life." She began to sob.

Brad put his arms around his wife and kissed the top of her head. "Just leave us alone for a minute, please."

Jillian rose and started for the kitchen. Faith followed. Jillian went to the refrigerator and removed a bottle of wine. She found a water glass in the cupboard and filled it.

She turned back to Faith. "Do you want some?" She asked, offering her the bottle.

"No, thanks. I'll just take a glass of water."

"Okay, Miss Goody-Two-Shoes. What do you have to say to me? Go on, it's crap on Jillian day. Let's hear from you, too. A girl tries to look out for herself, and everyone shits on her."

"I don't have anything to say to you. You're going to have to work this one out for yourself. You can either stand alone to deal with it, or you can join with your family and be part of a team. It's entirely up to you. The choice is yours, Jillian." Faith picked up her glass of water and walked out of the kitchen.

When Faith reached the den, the phone rang. Brad answered. "It's for you, Faith." As he handed her the receiver, he covered the mouthpiece. "It's Henry Thompson," he whispered.

When Faith hung up five minutes later, she shook her head. "The board meeting is set for three o'clock Monday afternoon. He talked to me about selling our stock again. He even said, that as a friend of Oliver's, and one who believed in his innocence, he would be willing to buy it from us. He quoted me a firm price of thirty-two dollars a share no matter what Monday brings."

"I think that might be a little less than the stock is selling for on the exchange right now," Brad said.

"Are you sure?"

Brad looked at her. "No. I'm not. It's close anyway. He's a good friend, but he could get into trouble with this, if he isn't careful. On the other hand, Henry could be using this as an opportunity to pick up some extra shares cheaply because he feels when this is over it will rebound."

"I don't really think so. He and Fran were wonderful when Oliver was having such a rough time of it," Faith answered pensively.

"True, but it is business," Brad continued. "Consider this, if you sell to him, he gains the control you, or I should say we now share." Their eyes locked as he concluded.

"I hadn't thought of that."

Aaron Whitley didn't get back to Faith until evening. Jillian had returned to Chapel Hill, and the rest of them had just finished dinner when the phone rang. Faith took the call in the den. She filled him in on what had transpired since they had last spoken.

"We've been talking among ourselves. Do you think that you could attend that board meeting with me? You are," she continued, "excuse me, you were Oliver's attorney. And, it appears that he's going to be accused of involvement in embezzlement. And, you're the trustee for Jillian's stock. I'd feel much more comfortable if you were there to hear whatever is said first hand."

"I'll check my appointment calendar first thing in the morning. I'll certainly try to make it if at all possible. Perhaps then I can better advise you on who would be the best council for you to hire to represent Oliver's interests. Criminal law is a bit out of my field. I'm basically concerned with wills, deeds and the like. But I'll certainly try to steer you in the right direction, Faith."

"Thanks, Mr. Whitley. The company is supposedly hiring a law firm to represent them and, Henry Thompson said, possibly try to resolve Oliver's situation, too. But I definitely agree that I need to secure an attorney exclusively to represent Oliver."

"You absolutely do!"

When Faith rose the next morning, she called her real estate agent, Barbara Fields. "Barbara, I'd like to make a counter offer on the house. When can we meet?"

"I'm pretty much tied up all day, this evening, too. I could see you tomorrow afternoon around two."

"That will be fine."

"I'll let the prospective buyers know. See you then."

Faith went downstairs and found Mary Jane and Taylor in the kitchen. Brad had already left for the day with the older boys, and the little toddler was finishing his breakfast.

"I hope you can put up with me for another day or two."

"Stay as long as you like. I love the company, and, I must admit, it's nice having another female in the house to even things out a bit."

"Barbara Fields called me with an offer on the Cayman Shores house last Saturday morning. It was a terrible offer, and I was going to reject it. Now, with all of this coming to a head, I'm going to make a counter offer. I don't know how much I'll have to spend before this is over, so I think I need to get my hands on all the cash I can. I could be in for a long, bruising ride."

Mary Jane dampened a paper towel and began cleaning Taylor's face and hands.

"I'm still having trouble coming to grips with it all. And I hate that you're being forced into these tough decisions on top of everything else you've been through."

"Me, too. I hate it for all of us. But most of all for Oliver." Faith shook her head sadly.

The board meeting convened at precisely three o'clock Monday afternoon in the conference room of Hargrave, Taylor and Thompson. Faith had purposely been one of the last to arrive. She didn't want to talk with anyone before the meeting began. Aaron Whitley had promised to meet her there as soon as he could break away from a prior commitment.

The only absentee from the entire board was the treasurer, John Merrill. Steven Taylor, who had been elected Chairman of the Board when Oliver's illness forced him to resign, called the meeting to order.

"I think we can dispense with the formalities we generally use and get right to the business at hand. As I'm sure all of you are aware by now, two of our associates have been accused of embezzling close to a million dollars over a span of approximately a year, give or take a couple of months.

"This morning, both John Merrill and Scott Hansen were served with arrest warrants in their respective offices here at Hargrave, Taylor and Thompson. The arrests were made following the screening of the case by the district attorney's office and a grand jury's finding that there was, indeed, probable cause. They were lead away in handcuffs. It was quite a dramatic scene, and, unfortunately, some members of the press were present, too.

"This came as a surprise to all but a few of us. From what I've been told, the magistrate will most likely release them on their own recognizance. Jason and Steven have been put under suspension without compensation. The announcement of a new treasurer will be forthcoming.

"Their case will be tried in criminal court. Hargrave, Taylor and Thompson is presently considering a civil suit against them to try to recover the stolen funds. As many of you may be aware, our court system is pretty log-jammed so this could be a very lengthy, drawn-out process, perhaps a year or even longer before the case is even heard. Naturally, we'd lie to see a timely resolution and will do what we can to push for one.

"None of this bodes well for our company name or for our stock. We've been closely monitoring the price of the stock all day. I'm sure it comes as a surprise to none of you that it's in a downward spiral." Steven Taylor paused to take a sip of water. He removed a linen handkerchief from his inside coat pocket and blotted his mouth.

He was a rather short, stocky, middle-aged man with more salt than pepper graying hair. He was balding on the top of his head, but his hair was still full around the sides and in the back. Looking at him now, Faith couldn't help but notice how much he physically resembled Friar Tuck from the Robin Hood tale. However, there was absolutely no similarity in their demeanor.

She returned her attention to her note taking. Faith had brought a small pad with her and was logging key points of the meeting for Aaron Whitley, who had not yet arrived.

"It is my belief," Steven Taylor continued calmly, "that, if people don't panic, we'll survive this whole situation keeping our losses at a minimum. However, if everyone runs out and begins dumping large blocks of our stock, it would be devastating. As you are all aware, our shares have dropped from sixty-seven dollars a share, over the last several quarters, to twenty-nine fifty when I last checked an hour or so ago. Earnings have been way down, and now I think we have at least part of an explanation as to why." His voice and manner were perfectly controlled as he spoke, his eyes shifting from one to another of the board members.

Good for you, Faith thought to herself. *The voice of reason; we need that now.* He inspired confidence in her, and, as she looked about the table, she saw that the other members looked reflective but relaxed. And nothing had been mentioned about Oliver. Perhaps what Fran Thompson had told her was nothing but a rumor.

There was a knock at the conference room door. The secretary, Patricia Marsh, stepped to the door and opened it. She had a brief conversation with the new arrival then stepped back to Mr. Taylor and whispered something.

Steven Taylor looked at Faith. "Your attorney, Aaron Whitley, is at the door. He says you asked him to attend this meeting."

"I did," Faith said. She flushed slightly.

"Well." His brows arched, he sounded hesitant. "I don't object if the others don't."

"I am also the trustee of the shares of stock held by Jillian Hargrave," Aaron Whitley told them.

There were some murmurs about the table as everyone agreed that Aaron Whitley should sit in on the meeting. He entered the room and a chair was pulled up to the table next to Faith. She passed him her notepad, which he glanced over quickly.

Several members asked questions about the meeting's disclosures that Steven Taylor was either unable or not at liberty to answer. Faith felt her stomach churning.

She desperately wanted this meeting to come to its conclusion with no mention of Oliver.

"Our firm has hired legal counsel to represent us and that brings me to the last of our agenda for today." He looked at Faith before he continued. His expression was grave. "John Merrill and Scott Hansen have accused Oliver Hargrave of manipulating them into this scheme. Both say that they were his unsuspecting pawns."

Faith's heart began to pound, her palms moistened and her throat suddenly felt dry and tight.

"That's absurd," she managed to say.

All eyes focused on her. She felt Aaron Whitley's leg against the side of her thigh under the table. She looked at him, and he nodded.

"I speak for Mrs. Hargrave and her family," Aaron said rising from his chair. "For Oliver Hargrave to be involved in such a scheme as the founder, CEO, Chairman of the Board and major shareholder of this company is highly suspect. No one would stand to lose more from such action than he or, in this case, his heirs. It sounds as if these two men are looking for a scapegoat, and who better than a man who is no longer alive." His eyes met Steven Taylor's. "I'd like to ask if you know of any concrete evidence to support their claims?"

"I wish I could be of help to you," Steven answered. "I can only tell you this. There is some pretty damaging documentation."

Damaging documentation! The phrase played over and over in Faith's mind. She heard nothing else that was said in the remaining few minutes of the meeting.

CHAPTER 21

As Faith drove back to the Allen house, it seemed as if the world were squeezing in around her. She felt as if she would suffocate from the weight of all that had happened to her in the last months, and now this new dilemma became just a continuation of that process. She felt that her entire life during the past year could be compared to a rapidly growing ball of snow speeding down the side of a mountain that stretched into a huge white abyss. When would it all end?

"What you need to do is fight harder," she said aloud. But it would help tremendously if she could learn what that damaging documentation was. Aaron Whitley had assured her that they would learn the answer. She would just have to be patient and allow the evidence to unfold according to the law. But Faith didn't want to be patient. She wanted answers. Immediately! She had spent too much of the last year and a half of her life standing helplessly by while fate called all of the important shots. She wanted desperately to be able to take some positive action, now, on her time schedule and resolve this entire awful nightmare.

And it certainly didn't sound to her as if there would be any defense of Oliver on the part of the company's newly hired legal team. That would be entirely up to her. She must find an excellent defense team.

Tuesday afternoon Faith met Barbara Fields in her office at the agreed upon time. Barbara handed Faith a copy of the offer on her home. "I'll give you a minute to read through this and see if you have any questions."

Faith finished reading and laid the contract down. "I can't believe anyone would offer that much less than the asking price."

"I've seen it before. Sometimes it works to their advantage," she said. "Sometimes, it doesn't."

Faith wrote in a counter offer and signed her name.

"I'll take this to them this evening," Barbara said putting the contract into a folder and placing it in her briefcase. "I know where to reach you. I'll be in touch."

As she drove to Mary Jane and Brad's, Faith thought of Laura. I need to call her. She had phoned her friend during the day on Monday but had only reached her machine.

Faith had left the message that she'd be staying in Winston-Salem indefinitely. She gave her Mary Jane and Brad's number again in case Laura needed her. She hadn't heard back. She hoped that didn't mean Laura was worse.

Over the next several days, Faith met with Barbara Fields two more times with counter offers to the potential buyers. In the end she agreed to let the house go for nearly twenty-five thousand under her original asking price. It made her angry to feel that she'd been placed in the position of having to accept the offer. But she needed to get cash in her hands. And she wouldn't be able to put that money against the beach property mortgage as Oliver had hoped she might. She was grateful to be able to keep the money that she had cleared from the transaction as Oliver had added her name to the deed. That was one asset that didn't have to go through probate.

She met with her new defense team, Mabry, Mann &Webster, on Friday morning. They were going to be expensive. She paid them a five-figure retainer, twenty-five thousand dollars to be exact. They told her that when that sum had been spent, they would assess her additional charges. She doubted that would take long as they had the reputation of being a pricey firm but excellent defense attorneys. No court date had been set as yet. Justin Mabry told her that if no charges were filed against the estate in the next week, then the bar-date would have passed for allowing claims against Oliver's estate. After that time, the courts would no longer have access to any of the estate. Faith left their offices feeling hopeful.

She was so exhausted that she decided to stay in Winston-Salem through the weekend. On Monday she would call Linda Hart to see if she would be interested in buying the business.

Most of Faith's waking hours on Saturday and Sunday were spent thinking about this new predicament and discussing it with Mary Jane and Brad whenever the children weren't within earshot. It filled her dreams at night, too.

Monday morning, she called the shop just after ten. Linda was in the habit of getting to work earlier now that she was in full charge. She answered the phone on the third ring.

"Oh, Rachel! Sorry, I mean Faith. I'm so glad you called. I apologize for leaving so many messages, but I need to talk with you."

"I'm in town, Linda. I've been here for over a week. So I didn't get any of your messages. I called because I'd like to come by and talk to you today whenever it's convenient for you."

"Come anytime. Come now, if you can. We have major problems!"

CHAPTER 22

And the snowball rolls on, Faith thought, as she drove back to the house from her meeting with Linda. The decorating business had had four cancellations of prospective clients since the previous Monday. Linda had said when the first call came in to cancel, she took it in stride. The woman had a legitimate excuse. But, as the calls continued, she felt that the cancellations were linked to the scandal that had hit the television news and newspaper last Monday and had continued to garner headlines on the front page as well as in the business section each day thereafter.

"All of this negative publicity is really hurting us, Faith. We need to come up with some damage control."

"You're right." But Faith had no answers today.

Most of the reporting had managed to mention Faith's name as Oliver's widow and the name of her business too. One woman who had signed a contract and made a deposit had asked for her money back. Linda wanted Faith's guidance on handling that one.

"Give her back the money, by all means," Faith had told her. "Hopefully this will die down when the media finds something new to jump on."

After those revelations, it came as no surprise to Faith that Linda was hesitant to enter into any agreement to purchase the business. Faith shook her head pensively. When and how would this all end? Every day the situation seemed to deteriorate further.

She wanted to go back to the beach but she had a meeting scheduled with the new attorneys on Thursday afternoon. Then she'd head back to her retreat. Perhaps, there, where she spent some of the happiest times in her life, her perspective would improve. And she agreed with Marcus; the beach was a place where she, too, could do some of her best thinking. The thunder of the waves crashing ashore and the perpetual ocean breeze combined to drown out all other sound much of the time. For Faith, it seemed to create an invisible barrier between her and the rest of the world. It gave her a sense of belonging and refuge she felt no where else. It nourished her spirit. Yes. She needed to get back home.

Friday morning, Faith rose early eager to be on the road to Myrtle Beach no later than ten o'clock. She managed to leave thirty minutes ahead of her schedule. The weather was beautiful, sunny with barely a cloud in the Carolina blue sky. She felt her spirits lift as she drew closer and closer to the beach and *Faith's Retreat.*

She turned into her driveway four hours after leaving Winston-Salem. She climbed the stairs, rounded the deck and headed for the front door. She paused for a moment, leaned on the railing and gazed out at the sea. She inhaled deeply of the wonderful salt air and relished the gentle caress of the wind about her body. How wonderful it felt to be home again. She would try to shut out of her mind for the evening, all of the cares that had plagued her in Winston-Salem.

Inside, she carried her luggage into the bedroom then went out to the kitchen and poured herself a Coke. She started out to the gazebo and noticed that she had two messages on her answering machine. She stopped and pressed play. The first was from Fran Thompson and had come in last week. Obviously the Thompson's had caught up with her back in town. She wouldn't return that call. The second was a message from her attorney, Jason Mabry. He asked her to return the call, saying it was urgent.

She put her drink on the coffee table and dialed his office. She only had to wait a moment to be put through to him. After formal pleasantries, Mabry told Faith that he had spoken with Aaron Whitley earlier in the day. Aaron told him that a summons against the estate and a formal charge against Oliver as a co-conspirator in the embezzlement had been filed earlier this morning.

"I thought we were going to make it by the bar date. The lawyers for the prosecution have obviously done their homework. We only had to make it through midnight, and you'd have been home-free. I'm sorry, Mrs. Hargrave."

"So am I." Faith felt a knot tightening in her stomach. "So am I."

"I'll be in touch with you soon. I'll need to meet with you again and begin our defense preparation."

"Let me know when. It would help if you could give me at least one day's notice."

"I'll have my secretary call you."

"Thank you," she murmured. They said goodbye.

Just hours to go, she thought, *less than twenty-four. Why couldn't they have waited? Why did all of heaven and earth seem to be against Oliver and her? What would the outcome of all of this be?* She didn't even want to hazard a guess in the frame of mind she was in right now. And, she didn't want to think about it any more today. Like Scarlet O'Hara in *Gone with the Wind,* she'd allow herself the same delusion. She'd worry about that tomorrow.

CHAPTER 23

Faith took a couple hours to settle back in, to try to relax and reflect on everything about the troubling situation she now found herself in. As much as she knew she had to face it, she wanted to get into her bed, cover her head with a blanket and make the world go away for at least a little while. She called Mary Jane and Brad and had a long talk with both of them. She put the receiver down, and before she could walk away, the phone rang again. Perhaps they had forgotten to tell her something.

It was Steven Taylor. "Faith, I don't know what to say. I'm so sorry. It's the hardest thing I ever had to do, but I had no choice. I had to include everything our in-house investigation uncovered. There is a logical explanation for all this. I'm counting on you and your lawyers to find it. You know I loved Oliver as a brother."

Faith believed him. She knew how much Oliver had liked and respected Steven. She could tell by his voice this was tearing him up.

A little later, she unpacked and put a load of laundry into the washer. She made herself a peanut butter and jelly sandwich and a cup of hot chocolate. She went out onto the deck to eat.

When she finished, she went into her bedroom and read Oliver's letter again. There was nothing, no clue whatsoever that could in any way implicate him in all of this. Surely, if he were involved, the homes would have been mortgage free. His finances would have been in much better shape, and there would have been greater assets. In thinking back over the time they had shared, there had never been even one word to make her suspect of any of his actions. He had rarely spoken of either John or Scott. Never called them. Neither man was part of their inner circle of friends. She read Oliver's ending requests for her to go on for them, and she felt her resolve strengthening.

"I will clear your name. I promise you," she whispered broken-heartedly.

She returned the letter to her dresser drawer and went back out onto the deck. The sun was still bright and the breeze warm. Faith decided to walk down to the pier. When she reached Laura's, she stopped to see if she was there and felt like joining her.

Laura grinned when she opened her door. "Welcome back stranger, I've missed you." She embraced Faith. "I was beginning to think you'd sprouted land legs and had given up on the beach."

"Nothing like that," Faith said. "You look like you're feeling much better than when I left you. I thought you might like to walk with me.

"At least ninety percent better. It took a couple of days to come back from that last bout. Then I went up to Wilmington for a few days. I'll grab a windbreaker and be right with you."

When they reached the pier they walked out to the end, climbed to the top level then sat down to rest. "There's a bit more activity here than when I left. I guess it won't be long before this area will be teeming with tourists," Faith observed.

"Probably. And that reminds me, Marcus is flying in Sunday afternoon and Uncle Charles and Aunt Jean are going to drive down to have dinner with us. I'd like for you to come too. I want you all to meet. I think you'll like one another."

"That sounds like a nice evening. I'd love to come."

As they returned from the pier, Faith told Laura a little of what had happened since they had last talked.

"That's incredible!" Laura said, wide-eyed. "How absolutely awful for you, Faith. What are you going to do?"

"I'm going to fight. I'm going to clear Oliver's name. This afternoon I've been racking my brain, trying to think what on earth they could have against him that would possibly implicate him. I guess what I need to do is go through all of his papers. Before I came back, I went to the Cayman Shores house to make sure I had brought everything possible down with me. I did find a small metal box in the wall safe in his office. I brought that along and I'm going to look through it later tonight. Then I'm going to go through everything I brought with me when I moved down here. Somehow I hadn't the heart to get into all of that before. Now, I have no choice, it's a necessity.

"I'm sure it won't be easy. You don't deserve to be put through all this.

Neither does Oliver. He was such a fine man."

Faith glanced at Laura as they stopped outside her home. Laura looked as if her thoughts were miles away.

"Why does life have to become so difficult and complicated for the good people?" Laura asked pensively.

Faith got the distinct impression Laura was not speaking only of hers and Oliver's situation.

Laura started toward her front steps, then turned back to Faith. "Go to Mass with me in the morning?"

"No. No. I'm not ready yet. But thanks for asking." And to finalize her refusal, she added, "But thanks for understanding why I can't, Laura." They had discussed Faith's feeling about church and God on more than one occasion in the recent past. Faith realized that Laura was offering support for her to return when she was ready. She was grateful that Laura didn't press her further.

That evening after dinner, Faith poured herself a glass of white zinfandel and carried it into the office. She took several folders and boxes out of Oliver's desk drawers and began to go through the papers. There were receipts, cancelled checks, liquidated stock statements, some tax papers, the girls' birth certificates, Jane's death certificate and so forth, all routine information. Nothing to either help, or hurt, Oliver's case.

At last she reached for the metal box that she had found in Oliver's wall safe in Winston-Salem. When she lifted it, she heard something roll inside. Her heart rate accelerated slightly in the hope of finding something useful as her last resort of the evening. She pressed the latch and lifted the lid to reveal a beautiful single pearl and diamond pierced earring sans the tiny metal slide that holds it on. It had apparently rolled out of a piece of cotton padded tissue paper that lay at the other end of the box. Also in the box was an inkpad, a rubber stamp and a small pad of white paper, nothing more.

Curious, Faith thought. Why would Oliver keep a solitary earring in the safe? It certainly wasn't hers. And why would he lock away an inkpad and a rubber stamp? She lifted the stamp and pressed it into the ink. Perhaps this would shed some light on the matter. She made an imprint on the pad of paper. It was simply their Cayman Shores address. Faith shook her head. It didn't make any sense to her.

She re-wrapped the earring securely in the tissue paper and put all of the contents back into the box. She slipped it into the bottom drawer of the desk. She had reached a dead-end for tonight. She felt drained and disappointed.

"Oh, well, you didn't really expect this to be easy, did you?" she said softly. "But how do you find something to clear someone who has done nothing wrong?"

Frankly, she had no idea what she was looking for, so how would she know if she found anything that would be useful? One thing she was certain of, she'd found nothing incriminating. For that, she was deeply grateful.

Her phone rang. She stepped into the living room and lifted the receiver. "Hello."

"Faith? Fran Thompson, here. Henry and I are worried about you, dear. How are you holding up under all of this?"

"I'm holding, thanks. I don't think I have much choice."

"I wanted to have you over for dinner before you left, but there was so much happening. When I called over to Mary Jane's this morning to invite you, she said you'd gone back to the beach."

"That was thoughtful of you, Fran. It was a busy week. I needed to get back home."

"Then it's definite. You're making the beach your permanent home?"

"Yes. I thought you knew the Winston-Salem house is on the market." Faith didn't feel much like talking tonight, and she didn't want to defend her motives to Fran. She felt far too tired and drained for that. And, Henry was part of the company that had accused Oliver. As much as she didn't want to, she was beginning to feel a little resentment toward them.

Fran didn't acknowledge Faith's last statement. "Dear, I hope you don't think for a minute than either Henry or I think Oliver had anything to do with this horrid mess. Henry said that Steven Taylor felt that in light of the evidence they had to include him. I have no idea what he meant by 'the evidence'. I'm absolutely positive it will all work out in Oliver's favor."

"Thanks," Faith said halfheartedly. "I hope you're right."

"Well, I won't keep you any longer. One other thing, though. I did want to let you know that Henry has been given the nod to take over as treasurer of the company."

"How nice," Faith murmured.

"Call on us if we can do anything to help you, dear."

"I will." Faith hung up.

She felt very irritated with Fran tonight, and she wasn't sure why. Certainly Henry had been supportive throughout Oliver's illness. In fact, toward the end, both he and Fran had been thoughtful enough to come to the house and sit with Oliver for short periods of time, when Mary Jane was tied up, so that Faith could take a little break. She never left him for more than an hour, and usually she only went into another room, or for a short walk in the neighborhood to get some fresh air.

Steven Taylor had stopped by often for short visits, too. That was all the help she wanted from someone outside the immediate family. She didn't want anyone there constantly. And she was able to get by without using Hospice until the last two days.

Her parents had also offered to come, but Faith turned them down. As much as Faith loved her mother, she knew from experience how situations like this upset her. Carol Inman went all to pieces when someone became gravely ill, and Faith didn't need that. And, selfish or not, she wanted this precious last time she would have Oliver with her, as much to herself as she could have it. Mary Jane and Brad stopped in often for short periods of time and were a great comfort. Jillian came occasionally. She was usually whiney and demanding. Faith actually found herself close to hating someone for the first time in her life.

Her thoughts returned to Fran Thompson. She and Fran had been quite good friends from the time they met. But lately, she felt nothing in common with Fran. In fact, recently she found herself thinking of the woman as pushy and intrusive. She had started to feel uncomfortable even talking with Fran.

Stop that! She mentally admonished herself. That wasn't like her. Was she becoming embittered because of all that had happened to her? Was she jealous of Fran because she still had Henry and her life appeared to be going very well? Perhaps Faith needed a little introspection. Suddenly, she didn't like the person she was allowing all this adversity to turn her into. She was letting circumstances affect her, get her down, instead of taking charge and effecting change in them.

She went into the bathroom, showered, dressed in her nightgown and got into bed. As she was falling asleep, the image of the earring appeared in her mind's eye. Could she have seen it on Jillian? She wasn't sure, but something seemed vaguely familiar about it as it faded dreamily from her consciousness.

When Faith arrived at the Halls' for dinner Sunday evening, Marcus answered her knock.

"Come in. Good to see you again," he said. "We're all out at the kitchen table."

She followed Marcus into the kitchen. "Faith, hello," Laura said. "Come meet our aunt and uncle, Jean and Charles Dixon.

The man, who appeared to Faith to be in his late fifties, was dressed in slacks, a sports jacket and a clerical collar. He rose from the table and extended his hand to her.

"We hear a great deal about you from our Laura. Glad to finally meet you. She's quite a fan of yours." He had a merry smile and a firm handshake. "This is my bride Jean. Jean Dixon," he said turning toward his wife. Not to be confused with the psychic," he added with a chuckle, "except when it comes to predicting me."

"Oh, so you're newlyweds," Faith said, smiling at Jean.

Jean's eyes twinkled as she laughed. "We're not. We've been married for over thirty years," she confessed. "Charles always introduces me that way."

"That's because it seems like only yesterday, my dear."

"I had no idea that you were a minister. If Laura mentioned it, it didn't register with me."

"I'm an Episcopal priest, have been for pushing thirty years now."

After the meal, Marcus and Charles excused themselves and went for a walk on the beach. The women tidied up the kitchen, and Laura started a pot of coffee to have with dessert when the men returned. As they finished and went into the living room, Jean excused herself and went into the bathroom.

"I guess I didn't mention that Uncle Charles was a man of the cloth," Laura said easing down onto the sofa. "He's my mother's younger brother. Dad is Catholic and mother converted to his church shortly after they were married. We're kind of a mixed family, I guess. Charles was always our favorite uncle; he and Marcus have really become closer than Dad and Marcus in the last few years."

That made sense, Faith thought. If Marcus is having personal problems and his father is unsympathetic, it's understandable that he would turn to a relative, whom he felt close to and who was also a minister, for counseling. "It's nice that Marcus is able to spend time with his uncle. Do you know how long he'll be able to stay this trip?"

"He hopes to spend at least two weeks. If all goes as planned when he left, he may stay even longer."

"I hope your uncle can be of to help him. Whatever is troubling him, seems very serious to Marcus."

"It is. It's quite a difficult situation. There is a lot to consider," Laura said pensively. "But, I know Marcus. He'll come to the right decision."

Jean rejoined them in the den and, shortly after, the men returned. They all went into the kitchen for coffee, German chocolate pound cake and homemade ice cream.

Thirty minutes and a second helping later, Charles pushed his chair back from the table, "I think we'd better head on up the road, Jean. If we wait much longer, I might fall asleep at the wheel."

"Spend the night," Laura coaxed. "What do you have to rush back for?"

"We didn't bring an overnight bag. And Charles has a meeting early in the morning. We'll come again while Marcus is here. If we can, we'll spend a couple of days next time."

"I'll hold you to that," Laura said, embracing each of them. "But I won't hold my breath. I know how busy you two stay."

Charles took Faith's hand. "We've enjoyed spending time with you."

"We'll look forward to seeing you when we come back," Jean added.

Marcus rose. "I'll walk out with you."

Faith started gathering up the dessert plates and coffee mugs and carrying them to the sink. "I'll rinse and you can load," she offered.

"Deal," Laura said. "We make an okay team, don't we?"

"We do. I like your aunt and uncle. They made me feel a part of your family."

"You kind of are," Laura said smiling at her. "I have a great brother; I could use a terrific sister, too."

As the girls were finishing up with the dishes, Marcus stepped back into the kitchen. "They'll call us after Charles checks his schedule. He's aiming for a couple days near the end of next week."

"I'll say goodnight, too," Faith said drying her hands on a paper towel.

"This past week has been a hectic one for me. It's going to take me more than one good night's sleep to recover from it." She started through the house toward the door.

"Let me walk you down the beach, it's nearly dark and tourist traffic is beginning to pick up. You don't need to go alone." He caught up with her at the front door and they headed down the beach together.

"It's a beautiful night, isn't it?" Faith said, as she looked up at the waxing moon. This is my absolute favorite time of year. It's a time of beginnings. It reminds me of a young child, so full of promise and potential. It's a hopeful time." It surprised her to hear herself confiding these feelings to Marcus. That was something she would have said in her past, not something she had even thought of in recent months.

"I feel that way too," Marcus said quietly.

They reached the front of Faith's cottage. "Thanks for the company, Marcus. I enjoyed meeting your aunt and uncle." She started up the stairs.

"Faith," Marcus said softly.

She stopped and turned back.

"Yes?"

"Go sailing with me tomorrow?"

"Yes." Faith said, to her surprise without a moment's hesitation. "I'd like that very much, Marcus,"

CHAPTER 24

Faith rose early the next morning. She wanted to make some calls before she and Marcus set sail. She had given herself a mental lecture before going to sleep last night. In essence, she had said, *"Get off your butt, and get busy. This inertia you've been allowing to dominate you, is doing no one any good, least of all, you. It isn't like you. What would Oliver think?"*

And so she rose, dressed, ate breakfast and was ready to make phone calls at nine o'clock to start looking for office space and contacts. She had set up four appointments, two to look at office space and two to meet with realtors when she glanced at the wall clock to check the hour. It was time to meet Marcus, but she felt good, the best she had felt in months. And she credited the positive action she had taken today for this feeling.

Marcus brought his large sailboat as near the shore as he could. Laura sat in a small rowboat with a picnic basket at her feet. "Come on, I'll row you out!" she called to Faith.

It pleased Faith that Laura seemed to be feeling so well these days. "Great," she said. "Are you going along?"

"No, no, no." Laura laughed. "I'm just contributing lunch. This is as far out as I go. I'm only wearing my land legs today. You two are on your own. I've always said Marcus and I are the perfect team. He masters the sea while I tend the shore."

"I can't argue with that." Faith knew that Laura had a fear of the ocean, and she surmised it was because she wasn't sure that she would be able to save herself should the need arise. "I'll tell you what," she said. "When we're safely back on shore, I'll treat everyone to dinner tonight. You can choose the place, Laura."

"You've got a deal. Now, smooth sailing or whatever it is you wish those who are about to embark on a journey at sea." Laura's eyes twinkled in the sunlight. She really seemed rested and happy these days.

Marcus offered Faith his hand as she stepped aboard. He turned the rudder, and they set out to sea. It was a perfect spring day. The sun was bright and the temperature perfect for a sail but the waters had not yet warmed fully from the chill of winter. Marcus seemed more relaxed today than Faith had seen him. She commented on it.

"The ocean has always been therapy for me. It's as if when I'm here at the coast with the sand and the water and the wind, I'm in another world, a pure place where nothing corrupt can reach me."

What an unusual choice of words from him, Faith thought.

He continued, "I used to have some of my best talks with God when I was out here. Sometimes, when I talk to him now, I wonder if he still hears me." He looked at her quite seriously. "I guess that sounds awfully melodramatic, doesn't it?"

Her expression was as solemn as his. "Not to me. I agree with you completely. It seems to be the only place I can find peace anymore, but not because of God. When Oliver was alive, even after he got sick, I found more tranquility here, at Faith's Retreat, than anywhere else. God was in His Heaven; I still had hope. But He wasn't listening to me. Oliver died. I don't seem to be able to talk to God anywhere these days."

"That had to be awful for you. Awful to have just found one another and to have to live with the fear that your days together might be so short. I'm sorry, Faith," he said softly. "I'm sorry for both of you."

A seagull swooped down toward their sailboat. "What are you doing way out here?" Marcus asked it.

Faith opened the picnic basket and removed one of the sandwiches. She opened the baggie and tore off a piece of crust. "You deserve a reward," she said, tossing the crust into the air.

The bird devoured it and continued to hover about their sailboat. Faith threw it another and another piece until she had given him a whole piece of bread. "I think we'll have to call him Jonathon, he has such spirit."

"It's quite unusual to see a gull out this far," Marcus said. "I think that's a good name for him." The gull flew back to them periodically throughout their sail, even after they no longer fed him.

It was a totally restful day for Faith. She felt so at ease with Marcus that before the day was out, she had confided even more of the details of the scandal that was invading her life to him than she had to Laura.

Over the next several days, Faith signed a lease on a small office space in a business park on Business 17, the highway that spans the beach area. It would be two months before the renovations would be completed and she could move in. That suited her needs. She met with several realtors and showed them her portfolio. She felt encouraged.

A few days later as she and Marcus came ashore from a sail on his catamaran, a tall woman with raven hair approached them from the direction of Faith's Retreat. As the woman raised her arm in a wave, Faith realized who she was.

"Jillian!" she said aloud. "What on earth does she want from me now?"

"So, that's the infamous Jillian Hargrave," Marcus said, sounding a bit amused.

"It is. I'd best go see what she's after. See you later." She left him and walked quickly toward Jillian. They met half way between the Halls' and Faith's beach house.

"Hello, Faith." Jillian's eyes were fixed on Marcus as he pushed the catamaran ashore.

Faith took hold of Jillian's arm and started for her beach house.

"Hold on a minute," Jillian said breaking her grip. "Who's the hunk? Introduce me," she said, as she began walking toward Marcus.

"He's the brother of my friend, Laura Hall. And, he's not available."

"Oh? Do you have a claim on him, Mrs. Hargrave?"

"Be serious, Jillian. No, he's…"

Jillian wasn't listening. In her tight green knit top and sarong style print skirt with its deep mid-thigh slit, she walked toward Marcus, wearing her warmest smile. "I think he's the one who can decide whether he's available or not," she called back over her shoulder, as she continued on toward the man and his boat.

Suddenly, Faith felt furious with Jillian.

CHAPTER 25

As Faith continued toward her house, she could feel the pulsing of the veins in both of her temples. Her face felt flushed, too. *What on earth is that girl up to now?* She wondered in exasperation. She climbed the stairs and walked through the gazebo toward the house. She stopped midway and returned to the gazebo. She took a seat with a view of Jillian and Marcus.

It wasn't long before Jillian started back toward Faith's Retreat. It was a graceful scene to watch. The wind blew her long, shining, black hair back from her face and whipped at her skirt, blowing the slit wider to further expose her long shapely legs. Her hips swayed slightly as she walked. *She truly is a stunning woman*, Faith mused. *Too bad I find it so hard to see her inner beauty.*

She glanced toward Marcus to see if he was watching Jillian too, but he was beyond her view. The couldn't help wondering what he had thought after meeting the girl. Faith rose and walked back to the house before Jillian reached the deck.

She stepped inside and caught a glimpse of her reflection in the foyer mirror as she passed through.

She stopped and inspected her face more closely. Her skin had begun to take on a rich tan from her time spent walking on the beach with Laura and sailing with Marcus. And her short, wispy hair looked a shade lighter than her normal golden blond. It made her eyes look even bluer. She finger-brushed her wind-blown hair back into place. Instantly, she realized that she was comparing herself to Jillian. *Why?* Why was she doing that? She hurried on into the living room, as she heard Jillian's footsteps on the deck.

"So, what's for dinner tonight, Step-mom?" Jillian asked letting the heavy front door slam shut behind her as she entered.

"I hadn't given it much thought. I wasn't expecting company," Faith replied, trying to hide her growing inner anger.

"I know, I should have called ahead. I'm meeting a friend down at South Myrtle tomorrow. I had a free day today, so I thought I'd come early and spend the night here if that's okay."

Since she really had no choice in the matter, Faith took a quiche out of her freezer and fixed them each a tossed salad for dinner. Jillian was actually cordial, and she talked about her classes as they ate. She didn't tell Faith whom she was meeting, but Faith assumed it was a man. Jillian had told her once that she didn't much like women in general and didn't spend much time with them. She had said Mary Jane was the exception. Faith was quite sure that Jillian placed her near the top of the list 'in the general group'.

After the meal, Jillian went out onto the deck. Faith joined her when she had the leftovers put away. The sun was just beginning to set, and the horizon was streaked with brilliant orange.

"It almost matches your front door," Jillian observed.

"Almost." Faith pulled her sunglasses from atop her head down over the bridge of her nose. She saw Jillian straighten in her chair and look down the beach. Faith turned to see what had captured Jillian's attention. Laura and Marcus had walked out onto their pier and were feeding the seagulls.

Jillian rose. "I think I'll take a walk," she said, moving toward their pier.

"I'll go with you." Faith caught up with her.

They stayed at the Halls' for more than two hours. Laura invited them in for hot apple pie a la mode. Faith felt uncomfortable throughout the entire evening. At one point, Laura had asked her if she was feeling well. Jillian, by contrast, was witty and talkative.

As they were leaving, Jillian stepped over to Laura to thank her. Marcus pulled Faith aside. "I had a call this afternoon and need to leave tomorrow. I'm going up to see Charles and Jean early in the morning. I'll fly out of Wilmington. I don't know when I'll get back again."

Faith wondered what had happened to cut his stay short by a week.

Jillian stayed up and watched a late movie on TV, but Faith excused herself and retired to her bedroom. She found it hard to fall asleep, so she turned on her bedside lamp and picked up a book. She had trouble concentrating. Her mind kept replaying the evening at the Halls'. How charming and vivacious Jillian had been, and how she, by contrast, had been so restrained. Her recall ended with Marcus telling her that he must leave. With the thought of him, she realized she was disappointed that he was going. They had become friends and confidantes. True, he hadn't allowed her to be much help to him, but he had certainly been a good listener for her. He offered her advice only when she asked for it, otherwise lending his ear, and she had found that therapeutic.

Jillian slept late the next day and left shortly after noon. Before she left she asked about the Cayman Shores house. "So, Mary Jane tells me you've sold the 'mansion'." She said snidely. "When do you get your money?"

"It won't close for another four weeks. And I don't know if Mary Jane told you or not, but I'm taking a loss. There's a mortgage to pay off and, in all probability, most of what's left will go to the defense attorneys."

"Humph," she said airily. "I still need that money I asked you for, Faith. I can't believe you can't spare a few thousand."

"What do you need it for?"

"I have some medical bills to pay."

"Are you ill, Jillian? Your medical insurance premiums are being paid by the trust."

Jillian shook her head and gave Faith an exasperated look. "Not everything's covered by insurance," she mumbled. She left the house letting the front door bang shut.

One thing about Jillian, Faith thought, feeling very annoyed, *she never leaves any doubt as to how she feels about anything.* Faith yanked the linens from the guestroom bed, tossed them into the washer and remade the bed with fresh linens from the hall closet. She did a general cleaning then went for groceries.

When she returned from shopping, Laura phoned. "I saw you ride by. When you finish what you're doing, come down for a drink and some snacks. I'm getting used to having people about the place, and it's way too quiet here today."

Before she left the house, Faith had another phone call. It was Jason Mabry, her defense attorney. He told Faith that a tentative court date had been set for August twenty-fourth. She was relieved; it was sooner than she had expected. She was eager for this chapter in her life to come to a positive conclusion.

She walked down to Laura's half an hour later. They sat on the screened porch. Laura had mixed them a vodka martini, and she brought out a tray of assorted cheeses and crackers.

"That Jillian, she's a character, isn't she?" Laura began. "Not exactly what I expected. She can be quite charming."

"What were you expecting?"

"I guess I wasn't expecting her to show up down here to visit you for one thing."

"That was a real surprise to me, too. She can be charming when it suits her."

After Faith said it, she wondered if her comment had sounded a little catty.

"She's a beautiful girl. I like her complexion," Laura said. "I've always wished I could get a deep golden tan, but all I ever do is burn."

"Oliver always said Jillian resembled her mother in looks, and Mary Jane inherited her mother's good temperament."

"She certainly had her eye on my little brother, didn't she?"

"Yes. She definitely did. Jillian leaves no doubt in anyone's mind as to how she feels about men." She found it a bit curious that Laura had so much to say about Jillian's visit. It was out of character for her. She wondered why. Could it be that Marcus had an interest in her? "What did Marcus have to say about Jillian?" Faith asked.

"Not much."

Faith felt a strange sense of relief. "Do you think Marcus is any closer to working out whatever is troubling him?"

"Has he confided in you about it, Faith?"

"No, he hasn't. He's very private about his life."

"I think he's close to resolving everything, but he's not the only one involved." Laura said. "I suspect he'll talk about it with you when he feels the time is right."

As Faith pondered her conversation with Laura, she found herself wondering what had gone wrong in his relationship. She had glanced at his left hand recently, his ring finger to be more accurate. There was no evidence that he had ever worn a wedding band, but then many men never wear one. What could possibly have caused them to have a problem? And how large was his family? He never spoke of them. How old were they? Did he miss them? She thought he did, because he seemed to enjoy the time he spent with Grant so much, and Grant had really liked him.

Faith met with several new real estate agent contacts over the next few days. She had a lot of feelers out and was hopeful that something good would come of at least some of them. What did her father always say? "If you ask enough people to buy, eventually someone will say yes." Her father was a small-tool salesman and a very good one. The thought of him reminded her that she needed to call her parents. They were concerned about her, and she hadn't talked to them in nearly two weeks. She'd call tonight.

For all that seemed to be looking positive from her efforts, she couldn't shake the feeling of melancholy that had been with her for the last several days. She found it a bit puzzling. Perhaps when she actually signed her first client her mood would change.

She had just finished taking her evening shower when she heard the phone. She slipped her nightgown over her head and went over to the bedside table. She lifted the receiver.

"Hello."

"Hello, there. I was about to give up on you."

"Marcus! How good to hear your voice!" Faith felt her spirits lift.

CHAPTER 26

Time passed, hours became weeks, and summer was upon them and still no firm date had been set for the trial. The days and nights grew hotter, and tourists flooded the beach area. Faith signed a contract with a young couple from the D.C. area to decorate their newly purchased penthouse condominium in posh *Maison sur la Mer*. She had asked Laura to let her show them some of her artwork. She thought several of Laura's paintings would be perfect for their living room and bedrooms.

Laura had been very hesitant, she didn't feel her work was worthy of being presented by a decorator for consideration. Faith had persisted, and Laura finally gave her two seascapes for the couple to consider. They had loved both and had been thrilled with Faith's work on the penthouse. They were lavish in their praise of her and had promised her referrals. She had to admit it felt good to work again after her long sabbatical.

Laura was awed by the sum Faith gave her for her paintings. She kept nothing for herself from the sale of the Laura's work. She hoped it would be a boost to Laura's confidence and an encouragement for her to continue painting. Faith felt her work showed enormous talent and sensitivity.

Faith made several trips back to Winston-Salem during this time to meet with her attorneys. She always combined her business with a couple extra days to visit with Mary Jane, Brad and the boys. She promised Grant and Christian to try to work out a time when they could spend a few days with her later in the summer.

She'd had no contact with Jillian since the day Jillian left in a huff. Though at time she had mixed feelings, she wasn't quite ready to give up on the girl. Oliver wouldn't want her to. Faith tried to phone her a couple of times but only reached her answering machine. She had left messages asking Jillian to return the calls, but had heard nothing from her.

The Cayman Shores house closed and after another payment to the attorneys, she had put the remaining cash into the highest yielding money market account she could find. It was a shamefully low return, but she needed to keep it liquid and penalty free.

Marcus hadn't been back to the beach since spring. Laura spoke very little of him. He called Faith on several occasions. Each time they had found it difficult to say good-bye. She found it comforting to hear from him, to hear his voice. She always felt a little sad after the call

ended. She finally had to admit to herself that she missed him. He had become a true friend.

She felt strangely elated when he told her he was planning to spend a few days at the beach in late July. As the date of his arrival neared, she found herself thinking of him more and more. As July approached, she became more and more curious about his life.

Laura asked Faith if she would drive her to the airport the day Marcus arrived for his short visit. Faith was pleased.

Faith's attorney had wanted to schedule a meeting with her on the day Marcus was to arrive. Without hesitation, Faith had told the secretary that she couldn't make it and had rescheduled to meet with him the following week instead. When she got off the phone with Jason Mabry's secretary, she admitted to herself what she had just done. She had rescheduled because she hadn't wanted to be away while Marcus was at the beach.

She and Laura arrived at the airport twenty minutes before the plane was due in. Faith felt a little giddy as they walked to his gate. When they checked the flight schedule, they found that his plane would arrive fifteen minutes late. They took a seat and waited. They finally saw the red light flash beside his flight number indicating that the plane had landed. Within moments, the passengers began filing into the airport waiting area. Laura and Faith stood as they waited for Marcus to walk up the ramp. A steady steam of passengers walked toward them. Marcus wasn't among them.

Laura looked at Faith. "I know this is the flight number he told me. And I know this was the day and time. I don't understand it. He would have called if anything had changed."

They waited a moment longer. No one else came up the ramp. They heard the announcement over the loud speakers that the passengers for that flight could begin boarding at the gate.

"This isn't like Marcus," Laura said. "Something is very wrong."

Faith mentally searched for the words that would reassure Laura, but couldn't come up with any. She was feeling equally concerned. And added to her worry, was disappointment.

"Let's go home and see if there's a message. He's probably left me a message," Laura said nervously.

They headed back for the main lobby. They hadn't gone far when they heard someone call their names.

"Laura! Faith!"

They turned and saw Marcus coming toward them. Faith's heart skipped a beat. Relief washed over her.

"Thank God," she whispered.

She remained stationary as Laura walked toward her brother. She watched them embrace and kiss. Marcus put his arm around his sister as they walked to where Faith stood. When they reached her, Marcus embraced Faith. She felt her arms encircle his neck. She felt his lips touch her forehead, and a strange electric sensation started in the pit of her stomach and spread throughout her body.

CHAPTER 27

"What took so long for you to get off that plane?" Laura wanted to know.

"I knew the pilot from college. Noah Wyatt. You remember him, Laura." She nodded.

"I saw him shortly before take-off, and I stayed on a few minutes after we landed to finish the conversation we'd started earlier."

"Well, you gave us a scare," his sister scolded.

"You're right. I apologize."

After Marcus arrived, time seemed to fly. He and Faith went sailing the following day, and, when Faith returned home afterward, there was a message from Mary Jane on her answering machine. She, Brad and the boys planned to come to the shore on Saturday and stay overnight, if that was convenient. Faith called her, and they made plans.

The Allens arrived around noon on Saturday. The boys were full of themselves! They couldn't change into swim trunks fast enough. Brad took the two older boys out on the pier while Taylor stayed behind with the women to take a nap.

"I hate to have to put him down right as we've arrived," Mary Jane told Faith. "But, if I don't, he'll be a real little beach crab."

They made plans to go out to dinner with Laura and Marcus. Brad was hungry for crab legs, and they had multitudes of seafood places to choose from during this, the peak tourist season. They decided on one of the Bennett's restaurants and had to stand in line for over half an hour to get a table large enough to seat the group.

The Allens and the Halls hit it off from the start. Marcus and Grant picked up where they had left off months before. Marcus promised to take the boy, and anyone else who wanted to go along for a sail after church the next day.

Sunday morning, they headed out to ten o'clock Mass together. It was the first time Faith had been inside a church in months. When Mass ended and the group walked out, Faith noticed that Marcus remained behind on the kneeler. It was several minutes before he joined them outside.

Back at the house, Brad, Grant, Christian and Marcus went sailing. Laura went home to rest while Faith and Mary Jane went inside to do a load of laundry before Mary Jane packed them up to leave.

"It's amazing how many changes of clothes three small boys can go through in a little over twenty four hours," Mary Jane said, as she folded the last little outfit and placed it in the suitcase. "I hope we didn't wear you out. The boys can be pretty rambunctious when they're excited. And, I do apologize for such short notice. We just decided on the spur of the moment."

"Don't be silly. I've loved every minute of it. You're family. This is your home, too. Come whenever you like."

"You seem to be doing so well, Faith. I think you've made the right decision in moving down here. It agrees with you. You look much more rested.

"Thanks. It has been a good move."

Grant and Christian bounded through the front door with Brad at their heels. "Can we stay for a few days, Mom? Please?" Grant begged.

"Can we, Mom? Can we? Just me and him?" Christian joined in the plea.

"Now what did we say about this before we left home?"

"Please, please!" Christian jumped up and down and landed in the middle of the off-white sofa in his wet swim trunks.

"Christian! Stand up! You're clothes are wet and that's a white sofa."

"He's okay," Faith came to the small boy's defense. "It's scotch-guarded. If it gets dirty, it'll wipe right off."

Mary Jane continued. "You know you both have places to go every day this coming week. And, remember, I told you that very soon Faith is going to come to

Winston-Salem. She'll be staying with us for a while, maybe even for several weeks.

The approaching trial came to the forefront of Faith's thoughts for a moment and a chill shot through her. She'd been trying to keep her mind off it as much as possible. She had mixed feelings about it. On the one hand, she welcomed the opportunity to address it and to finally hear what they thought was so damaging on Oliver's part. On the other, she was fearful of the outcome. So much depended on the jury selection, the skills of all of the attorneys, the length of time the trial dragged on. Even the judge who heard the case could have a powerful impact. There were just so many uncertainties.

She became aware of two sets of little arms hugging her waist and two little voice shouting noisy good-byes. She returned her attention to her family. And then suddenly, they were gone. She was alone again, and the house seemed to take on a deafening silence.

She went out onto her deck and walked to the gazebo. She needed to sit, to feel the ocean breeze gentle against her skin, to watch strangers play in the waves and seagulls in search of a morsel of food. To find anything to occupy her mind and rid herself of the sudden and vast aloneness she felt at their departure.

She didn't know how much time had passed as she sat there. Perhaps she had even napped; she wasn't sure. Someone called to her.

"Hey, lady, would you mind throwing us our ball?"

She looked toward her pier, and a brightly colored beach ball was blowing toward her. She rose and walked toward it, picked it up and threw it back to them. She walked down the stairs and out on to the beach. Before she realized where she was headed, she was at the Halls'.

"Come in," Laura called from the screened porch. "I take it your family has left."

"Yes. They've been on the road for a while now. The time passed so quickly, it was almost as if they blew in and right on through," she said with a smile. She climbed the stairs and took a seat in one of the chairs across from Laura.

"Where's Marcus?" she heard herself ask.

"He made a run to the grocery store." Laura glanced at her watch. "Should be back any time now. Stay and eat a hamburger with us. He's going to cook tonight; he's good with a gas grill."

The hamburgers hit the spot. After dinner they all walked down to the pier. They walked its length and climbed the stairs to the observation deck to sit and watch the sunset. A family of dolphins showed off for them a few yards away to the right of the pier. They were the first Faith had seen this season.

They started back down shore at dusk, but, before they reached their homes, darkness had descended. With only a crescent moon to light their way, Laura walked more slowly for fear of stepping into a hole created by the ebb and flow of the evening tide. It took nearly an hour for them to walk the distance. Laura was tired when they reached her cottage. She said goodnight and went in to take a shower and get ready for bed.

Marcus walked with Faith to her place. "It seems as if you just arrived, and now it's time for you to leave again," she said.

"I know," he nodded. "I had hoped we'd," he began, then stopped. "Your family's great. I'm glad I got to meet them."

"They really are. I don't know how I would have made it through these last two years without them." Had it really been that long since Oliver became ill? Had he been gone for over a year? It hardly seemed possible in one way, and yet, in the face of all that had happened during and since that time, she felt as if it had been an eternity.

"There's such a contrast between Mary Jane and Jillian," he said. "It's hard to believe they're sisters." He hadn't mentioned Jillian since he met her until now.

"Yes. They're like night and day," she agreed.

They had reached her door. "Thanks for dinner and the walk."

He put his hand on her shoulder then let it slide down her onto her outer arm before releasing it. "I hope it goes your way at the trial. I'll call you. You may need a friendly ear."

"Thanks, I hope you will. I try not to worry, but sometimes when I let myself think about it, it's hard not to."

"You're a strong woman, Faith." He leaned very close to her for a moment.

She gazed back into his eyes without speaking.

Suddenly, he turned and started toward the pier. "See you tomorrow," he called back to her.

"Tomorrow," she said softly. Her knees felt weak. *What's happening to me?* She wondered. Faith stepped through the front door and locked it behind her still feeling a little shaky.

CHAPTER 28

Faith, Laura and Marcus drove to the airport the next morning. Traffic was heavy and they barely made it in time. Marcus had to run to board his plane with only a waved farewell. For the second time in as many days, a feeling of loneliness sweep through Faith.

Her attorney's secretary called Faith and cancelled the meeting that had been rescheduled. Jason Mabry would likely be tied up in court on another case all week. He would call Faith one evening and go over some trial issues with her.

On Wednesday, much to her surprise, Faith had a call from Jillian asking if she could spend a couple days with her. She arrived Thursday afternoon.

She hadn't been there long when she asked, "So, where's the hunk? Mary Jane said he was here."

So that was it, Faith thought. *She must be between men.* "He lives in Philadelphia, and he's gone back."

"Hmmm." She looked disappointed. "So, what's for dinner tonight?"

"I have some steaks in the refrigerator. How does that sound?"

"Sounds great. Want me to wash some potatoes for you?"

Faith got a couple of potatoes out of the vegetable drawer and handed them to Jillian. She got out the fixings for tossed salad and, after Jillian washed the potatoes, she actually helped Faith chop some of the vegetables for the salad, then, went on to set the table for them.

It amused Faith. *Now what's she up to?* she wondered.

Jillian was fairly pleasant company for the entire evening. They watched a video together before retiring.

Jillian slept later than Faith on Friday morning. When she came out for coffee, Faith was ready to leave for an appointment.

"I tried not to wake you," Faith said. "I shouldn't be more than an hour. Coffee's made, there's cereal in the pantry, you know where the bread is, and there are bacon and eggs in the fridge. Make yourself at home," she said, as she stepped through the door. Faith had a verbal commitment to decorate a home a couple of miles down the beach, and she was going to meet with the owners and sign the contract this morning.

As she drove, she reflected on her turn of fortune. She was grateful that her business was beginning to pick up down here. It was a validation of her talent. The Winston-Salem business had fallen off dramatically. In fact, she and Linda had even discussed closing down under the present name and Linda reopening in another location under a different business name. She had let the part-time help go, and Ron Jefferson now worked only as a freelancer. That was the bad thing about working with the clientele she had acquired through her contacts. They were very cliquish. All had been great until the scandal broke, at which time they had deserted her en masse.

Her business didn't take as long as Faith expected. In less than an hour, she was headed back home. She climbed the stairs and went into the house. There was no sign of Jillian. She must be down on the beach, Faith thought. She went to her bedroom to change her clothes and join Jillian. Her bedroom door was closed. As she turned the knob she heard noise inside the room. She pushed the door open.

"Jillian!" Faith cried. "I don't believe this! How could you?"

CHAPTER 29

Jillian gasped. She pushed the dresser drawer shut with one hand and drew her other hand behind her back as Faith stepped into the room. "I was... I was just... I was looking for.... Oh, shit! I was looking through your drawers."

"And what do you have behind your back, Jillian?" Faith stared straight into Jillian's eyes. She already felt she knew what the girl had in her hands.

Jillian's face was beet-red, and she was breathing heavily. She brought her hands back to the front of her, revealing the letter. "It's the letter Dad wrote you, the one Aaron Whitley gave you after the will was read."

"And, have you finished reading *my* letter, Jillian?"

The color was fading from the girl's face, and her breathing had slowed.

"I read it once. I was reading it again when you came in on me."

Faith held out her hand for her letter. Jillian reluctantly placed it on her palm. "Then, you really didn't have anything to do with my trust, did you? It really was all Dad."

"That's right, Jillian. I knew nothing of how he had arranged his finances until the will was read. We had never discussed money after he became ill. I never wanted him, not even for one minute, to think that I didn't believe he was going to get well."

"And you truly never did tell him how I treated you either, did you?"

"I told you long ago, Jillian, that was strictly between us."

Jillian looked crestfallen, as if she might cry. She walked over to the bedroom door before turning back to Faith. "I have to think about this," she said. "I think I might have misjudged you after all." She went to her room.

Faith felt a bit shaken and surprised at Jillian's reaction to finding the letter. She had never seen the girl appear this vulnerable, not even when Oliver died.

Faith refolded her letter, put it back into the envelope and placed it in her dresser drawer. She straightened some of the garments Jillian had rumpled and closed the drawer. She left her bedroom and went out the living room.

When Jillian reappeared a few minutes later, she carried her suitcase and had her car keys in her hand. "I need to leave now. Thanks for letting me stay with you."

Then she did something that amazed Faith. She walked over to Faith and embraced her tightly for a long moment.

Faith had tears in her eyes as Jillian left. She thought Jillian's looked a bit misty too.

CHAPTER 30

The week before the trial was to start; Faith packed two suitcases and her cosmetics bag and left for Winston-Salem. She met with her attorney the day before the trial was scheduled to commence.

Faith, Mary Jane and Brad arrived at the courthouse thirty minutes early on August twenty ninth. By three o'clock, the case still hadn't been called. Sitting and waiting made the time drag. Faith had brought a book to read, but she found it hard to concentrate. Eventually a clerk came out and told them that they could leave for the day and to come back the following morning.

It was another two days before jury selection finally began. That was a fairly arduous process. More than sixty men and women were questioned before the final juror was selected. Once they were seated and charged, the balance was tipped to the female side, with eight women and four men. Both of the alternates were women.

The courtroom was nearly full and buzzed with conversation as Judge Daniel Braswell rapped his gavel, signaling the spectators to come to order. There were several people in attendance from Hargrave, Taylor and Thompson, including Fran and Henry Thompson. They took the bench behind Faith as the row she was seated in was full by the time they arrived. Fran reached forward and gave Faith's shoulder a squeeze as they settled in.

There were the usual opening statements by both sides before the prosecution began calling witnesses. Things proceeded slowly and, to Faith, seemed to be a great deal of repetition.

When the morning session broke for lunch, the Thompsons asked Faith to join them. She didn't particularly want to but couldn't think of a reason not to. As she sat across the table from her, Faith couldn't help but notice something different about Fran.

What was it? *Had she lost some weight? No, it was something about her face, a face lift perhaps?* Faith thought she was too young for that. She was dressed to the nines, but that was usual for Fran. She certainly looked rested. Perhaps that was it. Lunch had been pleasant enough.

The trial started Friday afternoon. Not a great deal was accomplished in the few hours until court was recessed for the weekend. Jason Mabry and Faith spoke in the hall at the end of the day. He had received a list of the items that would be entered into evidence. It appeared that there were a number of checks signed by

Oliver that had been deposited into the checking account of a bogus company.

Because Taylor's chest was congested and he was running a fever, Mary Jane hadn't been in court. Brad hadn't been able to sit in either because of business obligations. Faith left the courthouse feeling very disturbed.

After the boys were in bed Friday evening, Faith relayed what her attorney had learned of the evidence against Oliver to Mary Jane and Brad. The trial proceedings were the major topic of conversation throughout the weekend.

"I won't believe this of my father. He was a stickler for honesty his entire life. No, he wouldn't do such a thing!" Mary Jane said adamantly.

"Mary Jane's right. It would be totally out of character for him," Brad agreed.

"I'm going to ask Jason Mabry to put me on the stand. I want to testify. And I also want to see the evidence with my own eyes," Faith said resolutely.

Jillian called on Sunday afternoon. She spoke to Mary Jane for a few minutes then asked for Faith.

"I just called to see how it is going?"

"It's going. That's about it. Things are pretty slow. There was a two-day delay in getting started. Then it took a while to select a jury. When they finally got on with matters, it was only a few hours until court recessed for the weekend."

"Do you have any feel for how it looks for Dad at this point?"

"No. Not really."

"Okay. Let me talk to Mary Jane again."

"Thanks for calling." Faith shook her head slightly and handed the phone to Mary Jane. Where was the brief flash of warmth they had shared a short while back? Still, she had asked to speak to her.

Monday morning Taylor was still running a fever, so Faith went alone to the courthouse. Mary Jane was apologetic.

"I hate for you to have to face this alone."

"There's not a thing you can do sitting in the courtroom. I understand, and I'm fine. Don't give it another thought."

Wednesday morning, John Merrill took the stand. He was sworn in then questioned by his attorney. He testified that Oliver had called him into his office shortly before they learned that Oliver was ill.

"And what did he say to you, Mr. Merrill?" his attorney asked.

"He said that he was setting up a branch of the company under the name

O. H. Gravely. He told me that he would be shifting funds into that company from time to time."

"Did you find this at all unusual?"

"No. But what I did find unusual was the fact that he said his would be the only authorized signature on the account."

John Merrill's attorney finished his preliminary questioning twenty minutes later. Then it was Jason Mabry's turn. He rose and approached the witness.

"This company, O.H. Gravely, did you ever mention it to anyone else at Hargrave, Taylor and Thompson?"

"He... Oliver Hargrave, asked me to keep it in confidence. Said we'd just see how it went before he brought the others into it."

"And so you told no one of this little venture of his?"

"Well, as I became concerned, I did talk to Scott Hansen at length on several occasions. He's my brother-in-law and a close friend, as well as a junior partner at the firm."

"Is he the only person you shared this information with?"

"Objection," Your Honor," his attorney said, as he rose from his seat.

"Over-ruled. You may answer the question, Mr. Merrill."

"Well...yes...no... He's the only one." He glanced nervously out into the courtroom.

"Who was that other person?" Jason Mabry pressed, picking up on what he perceived as John Merrill's near slip.

"He...Scott was the only one. There was no one else," he said, glancing into the courtroom again.

Faith felt a little pang of electricity streak through her. She looked in the direction that John had. As the courtroom was crowded, she had no idea whom he had looked at. There was murmuring in the courtroom. The judge reached for his gavel.

"We'll have no more outbursts in this courtroom," he said sternly. "Or I'll clear the courtroom." He gave another rap with the gavel. "Proceed."

The room quieted. The testimony continued. When John Merrill left the witness stand and took his seat, Scott Hansen was sworn in. Scott was still being questioned when court recessed for the day. When Faith turned to leave, the Thompsons were nowhere to be seen. For an instant, she found herself wondering if Henry could possibly have been the person John looked at, when he'd said "he." John had looked in Henry's general direction. And now, Henry and Fran were gone. Why had they left early? Was she being paranoid?

Faith had a terrific headache by the time she reached the house. She took a couple of ibuprofen and drank a cup of black coffee while she filled Mary Jane in on the events of the day.

"I feel so upset these days. I find myself beginning to feel suspicious of everyone. As if the whole company has betrayed me. As if they've been deceptive…and I'm not exactly sure why. But I hate feeling this way."

As she lay in bed that night, sleep eluded her. She tossed and turned, and her thoughts kept returning to the Thompsons. The image of Fran during their lunch together, kept popping into her thoughts. It plagued her throughout her fitful night's sleep. As she awakened the next morning, it was in her thoughts again.

The next day turned out to be a short day of testimony, as Scott Hansen became ill on the stand. He was experiencing chest pain, and his color looked awful. The judge called a recess until the following day. Again, the Thompsons left before Faith had a chance to speak to them, and she was curious as to why. She wondered honestly, if she did have a chance to talk to them, what she would say.

Perhaps she should ask Jason Maybry's advice on the matter. She did. He told her to say nothing to them. He didn't understand why she felt the need to speak to them at this point.

He gave her a puzzled look. "Perhaps you need to stay away from court for a day.

I think the strain is beginning to get to you.But, for your information, Henry Thompson's name has been added to the list of witnesses," he told her. "Henry will be a general witness for the company. Please don't say or do anything to endanger what he could do to help Oliver."

Faith gave him a slight smile. "Thanks for telling me. You're right, I know my nerves are on edge these days. I certainly wouldn't want to do anything to hurt Oliver.

Marcus called her that evening. It was wonderful to hear from him. They talked for nearly two hours. When they hung up, Faith felt much better.

During the next session of court, Scott Hansen was able to return to the stand and finish his testimony. The next witness was called.

At two-thirty in the afternoon, Henry Thompson raised his right hand and swore on the Bible to tell "the truth, the whole truth and nothing but the truth, so help me God." He never looked in Faith's direction. His testimony continued until five o'clock. He was saying nothing to change the theory of Oliver being involved. Faith felt angry with the Thompsons, angry and deceived. Interestingly, Fran who had faithfully attended each prior session was noticeably absent from the entire day's proceedings.

Faith focused her attention on the jurors. She found herself studying their expressions as she listened to Henry Thompson damage Oliver's reputation. Henry was a handsome, self-assured man and, as he spoke quietly, Faith felt that some of the women on the jury were buying his story. Some of his 'recollections' were intentional lies. She knew that for a fact.

At a brief mid-afternoon recess, Faith huddled at their table with Jason Mabry and his assistant.

"I had a premonition about this," Faith said on the verge of tears. "You should have listened to…"

"This isn't looking good for Oliver," Jason cut her off mid-sentence. "But this is no time to get upset and argue among ourselves. We need to stay cool and react wisely. Henry Thompson is a very convincing witness. It's beginning to look very much to everyone as if Oliver did set up a corporate shell to funnel monies in and out of. We need to come up with something concrete to discredit these witnesses. Time is running out."

"But Henry Thompson is lying, and I don't know why."

"What proof do you have? Give me some proof."

Faith went home feeling angry with her attorney and the lowest she had felt since the trial began.

The following morning Henry took the stand and continued his testimony. Again, Fran was absent from the courtroom. After the lunch break, as Jason Mabry rose to cross-examine Henry, FranThompson entered the courtroom and sat down across the aisle from Faith. She never once looked in Faith's direction but stared straight ahead at Henry.

Faith kept glancing Fran's way. Henry reversed himself on one of the minor points that he had made earlier. Faith glanced over at Fran assessing her reaction. She stared long and hard at Fran for a moment.

Suddenly, her eyes focused on it. And then it hit her! The thing that had been troubling her about Fran since the day they ate lunch together. She thought she had the answer to all of this! It was all there. It was flooding through her mind. And it made perfect sense.

She must speak in private with Jason Mabry the moment court recesses.

CHAPTER 31

Faith and Jason Mabry went back to his office at the end of the day.

"I want to be called as the next witness," Faith said excitedly. "Can you arrange that?"

"I'll try. Why?"

"Just trust me," Faith said quietly. "I need to get a look at those checks. Then I want you to ask for a recess. Try to get us a full day, but, if you can't, take what you can get. I just need time to check on something locally and to get to the beach and back before court reconvenes."

"Just what do you have up your sleeve, Faith?"

"I think I know how to clear Oliver!"

"That's not good enough! I have to know where you're going with this, Faith."

He sounded annoyed with her. "That *is* what you hired me for, isn't it? Have you been withholding evidence from me?"

"I have! But only because I didn't know I had it!" Faith felt elated, excitement coursed through her veins.

She spent another hour with Jason Mabry filling him in on what she thought she had figured out.

CHAPTER 32

On Thursday afternoon, two weeks into the trial, Faith Inman Hargrave took the stand to testify in her husband's defense. Jason Mabry read from his list of questions for her and she answered each clearly without hesitation. Finally, the moment arrived that she had been waiting for. Several of the checks paid to the order of O. H. Gravely and endorsed by Oliver Hargrave were introduced as evidence. She was the first of the witnesses to be shown the "damaging documentation." This obviously was what Steven Taylor had referred to at the board meeting.

After the judge had been shown the evidence and the clerk of court had entered the checks into the record, Faith was allowed to examine them. Within moments, Jason Mabry requested a postponement until Monday.

The judge called the lawyers to the bench. After a brief consultation, a recess was called until Friday afternoon at two p.m.

"That's all the time I'm going to allow you," Judge Braswell said gruffly. "There have been too many delays in these proceedings already." He rapped his gavel firmly on his desk and left the courtroom wearing a frown.

It was three-thirty in the afternoon. Time was of the essence. Faith called Mary Jane on her cell phone. "Can you meet me right away? It's urgent!"

"Taylor is just waking up from his nap."

"Bring him and I'll watch him in the car." She quickly asked her a couple of questions then explained exactly what she wanted Mary Jane to do. Faith gave Mary Jane the address.

They met at four-fifteen in the parking lot of a small strip mall. Faith sat in the car with Taylor while Mary Jane went into one of the elite shops in the center. Twenty minutes later, Mary Jane left the shop and joined Faith in the car. She was smiling.

They drove back to the house and went inside. Faith packed an overnight bag and headed out for Faith's Retreat. Everything was going as she had hoped; she felt elated. Partway there, she turned the CD player on and sang backup for Celine Dion. She hadn't felt this charged in months.

When she reached the beach house, she dashed up the stairs, around the deck, inserted her key into the lock and let herself in. She ran to Oliver's desk and pulled out the bottom drawer. She reached in to remove the metal box. It wasn't there!

CHAPTER 33

Faith's heart sank. She dropped to her knees and began pushing the papers in the drawer aside. Finally she removed them all and scattered them about the floor. This was where she'd left the box. Had she realized how important it would become, she'd have locked it up. She began pulling all of the desk drawers out and rustling through the papers and folders.

When she had emptied the contents of the entire desk, she leaned back against a chair and began to sob. "Oh, God, why? Why don't You ever help me anymore?"

What happened to that box? She racked her brain trying to think where it could be. She went out into the living room and looked about. There was no sign that anyone had been inside. The cottage looked exactly as she had left it nearly three weeks ago.

She phoned Laura. After a moment of pleasantries, she asked, "Have you seen anyone around my place recently? Stranger…family, anyone at all?"

"No. No one other than tourists, but they were on the beach. I haven't seen anyone around the house."

Faith's mind was already off on another track. She'd given herself the clue. She had said family. Jillian had been there, going through her drawers. She thanked Laura and said good-bye.

Racing into her bedroom, she opened the top dresser drawer. Her letter from Oliver was right where she'd left it. She began removing the undergarments that filled the drawer. At the very back under a stack of nightgowns, her hand touched a metal object. She lifted it out. She held her breath as she raised the lid praying that the contents would be as she'd left them. They were!

Faith said a prayer of thanks. It had been so long since she had prayed that it felt strange now, yet comforting. And, God *had* answered her need.

She decided to stay over, get a good night's rest and leave very early in the morning. She would be back in plenty of time to meet with Jason Mabry well before court convened that afternoon.

She called Laura back and invited her to come for dinner. When Laura arrived a half an hour later, Faith realized that she had nothing much to fix a meal with. They decided to order in a pizza from Papa John's.

While they waited for their delivery, Faith began filling Laura in on the events of the last weeks. Laura listened mesmerized, as Faith concluded with her discovery and how she and Jason planned to use it in court tomorrow.

"Come back with me, Laura. Be there in court when we give them all their due."

"Oh Faith, I wish I could. But I don't know if I can be ready to leave that early."

"I'd love to call Marcus and tell him what I've found," Faith said, her eyes dancing. She noticed the amused look Laura gave her. "But maybe I'll wait, my phone could be tapped. Do you think I'm getting paranoid? "

Faith made it back to Winston-Salem well before noon on Friday. Laura had wanted to come but didn't want to slow Faith down. And Faith had running to do once she reached town. She made Faith promise to call her as soon as the trial, or at least Faith's part of it, was over.

Faith went directly to Jason Mabry's office. Jason had also done his homework. They were ready when they arrived at the courthouse a little before two that afternoon. Judge Braswell entered the courtroom, and Faith took the stand.

Jason Mabry stood and addressed the judge. "Your Honor, if it pleases the court, I have no further questions for this witness at the present time. I'd like to reserve the right to recall her if need be."

The judge looked at him quizzically. "Granted," he said.

"Your Honor, I would like to call Steven Taylor to the stand. I ask to have it entered into the record that he will be appearing as a witness for the defense of Oliver Hargrave."

The courtroom buzzed with whispers but, with the rap of the judge's gavel, quieted quickly. Steven had taken the stand earlier for the prosecution. He rose from his seat in the gallery and took the witness stand. Judge Braswell reminded him that he was still under oath.

"Would you please restate your position at the company for the record?"

Steven complied.

Then Jason Mabry asked for several of the evidentiary checks and handed them to Steven Taylor. "Mr. Taylor, you testified earlier that you worked closely with Oliver Hargrave for more than eighteen years. Is that correct?"

"Yes. That is correct, Sir."

"Would you examine these checks please, taking care to notice both the signature and the dates the checks were written." He handed them to Steven Taylor, who looked at each of them, then handed them back. "Would you agree that they bear Oliver Hargrave's signature?"

"Yes, sir. I've seen it many times. That is Oliver Hargrave's signature.

"Would you also agree that a signature stamp was used to imprint his signature onto this check?"

"Yes. I would agree. Several of us use a signature stamp."

"Who was responsible for the security of these stamps?"

"Why, each of us who used them."

"Could you tell me who at the company used a stamp?"

"Yes. That would be myself, Oliver Hargrave and Henry Thompson." We were each responsible for keeping our own."

"And after Mr. Hargrave became gravely ill and could no longer perform his responsibilities at Hargrave, Taylor and Thompson?"

"Let me think," Steven Taylor said. "At first, Oliver kept it at home with him. He kept it in his safe. He brought it with him when he was up to coming into the office. Then he became too weak to come in. And his eyes had failed him terribly. I believe once he no longer was able to come in at all, he still kept it in his possession."

The prosecutor objected. "Your Honor, this is supposition on Mr. Taylor's part."

"I'm going to allow the testimony to stand." And to Steven Mabry, "You may continue."

"Thank you, Your Honor. I have no further questions."

Steven Taylor left the stand and returned to his seat.

Jason Mabry remained standing. "I would now like to call Frances Thompson as a witness for the defense."

The prosecutor jumped to his feet. "Objection, Your Honor!"

"On what grounds?" Judge Braswell asked, with raised eyebrows. He motioned both of the lead attorneys to approach the bench.

They complied. Jason Mabry spoke in hushed tones. "Evidence has just come into my possession that makes

Mrs. Thompson's testimony extremely relevant, Your Honor." They all conferred for a moment longer before returning to their seats.

The judge rubbed his chin as he reflected, then said, "Overruled. You may proceed, Mr. Mabry."

Fran appeared completely shocked. Faith watched as she rose and walked a bit unsteadily to the stand. Her hand trembled slightly as she was sworn in.

Jason Mabry flashed her a disarming smile. He began speaking softly, asking very general questions until she appeared to have recovered somewhat from the initial shock of being called to testify. Her voice became increasingly calmer and steadier as she answered him.

Mid-sentence, Jason appeared to lose his train of thought. "Those are quite lovely earrings you're wearing, Mrs. Thompson. Might I inquire as to where you purchased them?"

"Thank you." She smiled at him. "They were given to me by my husband when he became a full partner in the firm. He had them specially made for me. There are no others like them."

Again, the prosecution objected. And this time Jason Mabry was reprimanded.

He asked several inconsequential questions of her before he said, "During the later days of Oliver Hargrave's illness, did you ever spend time with him so that Mrs. Hargrave could have a short break?"

"Yes. I did. We thought the world of Oliver. *And* Faith," she added quickly. We wanted to help in any way we could."

"Were you ever alone with Oliver Hargrave?"

"Occasionally, for very short periods of time. I don't see what this has to do with anything." She was becoming annoyed.

"Please bear with me a moment longer." Jason Mabry glanced at the judge, who gave him a curious nod. "Mrs. Thompson, did your husband, Henry Thompson, ever accompany you?"

"Of course, he did."

"To the best of your recollection, did he ever spend time alone with Oliver Hargrave?"

Fran was beginning to appear nervous. Her face flushed. Her neck and upper chest took on a blotched appearance. "I suppose he did occasionally. I don't know."

"Did you ever lose one of your earrings, Mrs. Thompson?"

"No," she said quickly in a high pitched tone.

"Did you ever go to First Freedom Bank to secure paperwork to open an account in the name of O. H. Gravely?"

"No. I did not," she said firmly.

"Did you return that paperwork, complete with corporate seal and the signature of Oliver Hargrave?"

"No. I did no such thing!" She struggled to appear composed.

"I suggest that you did, Mrs. Thompson. Oliver Hargrave's first symptoms were terrible headaches accompanied by blurred vision."

Fran was staring at him in wide-eyed silence.

"I suggest that your husband had Oliver sign several checks in the early stages of his illness, which you used to set up this account. I further suggest that the two of you went to Oliver Hargrave's home on numerous occasions on the pretext of relieving Mrs. Hargrave for an hour or so to gain access to his signature stamp until he became so ill that you thought he wouldn't notice. I suggest that at that time, you, Mrs. Thompson, took his signature stamp and left one containing his address in its stead. And, that at that time, you lost an earring. I further suggest that Oliver Hargrave, finding it and recognizing it to be yours and of significant value, put it into his safety deposit box to return to you at a later date."

"No. No! That's not true!" she proclaimed adamantly.

The attorney for the prosecution rose. "I object, Your Honor. He's badgering this woman."

"Sustained. Mr. Mabry, this woman is not on trial."

"I apologize, Your Honor. But, I believe that I can prove everything I've said today, if you will just bear with me a moment longer."

The judge nodded. "Then you may proceed."

He turned and walked back to Faith and she handed him something. He stepped back to Fran Thompson.

"Mrs. Thompson, I'd like for you to examine this earring and tell me if it is the one you lost a year and a half ago?"

She accepted the earring from him with trembling hands. She stared at it in silence.

"I personally have spoken with your jeweler, Mrs. Thompson. He has confirmed that he did indeed have to replicate one of your earrings approximately a year and a half ago. I have a copy of the insurance claim for the missing earring, which I am entering as evidence." Dramatically, he turned toward the jury and held up a piece of paper for them to see.

He turned back to his witness. "Mrs. Thompson, did you represent yourself as Oliver Hargrave's secretary when you secured the paperwork to open a corporate account in the name of O. H. Gravely?"

"No!"

"Wasn't your husband, in fact, representing himself on the telephone as Mr. Hargrave? And you didn't learn of Oliver Hargrave's demise until the day after he died."

"No! No! That isn't true!"

"Your Honor, I have documentation from Freedom Bank showing a telephone transaction made in the name of Oliver Hargrave on the morning after his death." Jason Mabry walked to his briefcase, removed several papers and asked that they be entered as evidence.

"In addition," he continued. "I…"

Fran began to sob. The courtroom erupted with gasps and murmurs. For the first time since Oliver became ill, Faith felt sheer exhilaration. She barely heard the rest of the proceedings.

Faith slipped out of the courtroom as soon as she could to call Mary Jane and tell her that it had worked and to thank her for her part in it. Mary Jane had gone into Bartholomew's Fine Jewelers on the pretext of having some earrings designed. She had told the jeweler that Fran Thompson had referred her to them. She casually mentioned how pleased Fran had been when they had replicated her lost earring, and the clerk had acknowledged that fact and had been pleased at her lavish praise of their work. That had made Jason Mabry's follow-up visit a mere formality.

"You helped our case tremendously," Faith told her. "If I had gone into the jewelers, I'm afraid they might have recognized me and connected me to the trial. I don't know if it would have made a difference in their openness or not, but I didn't want to take a chance. I think all of this has made me paranoid."

"Oh, Faith, this is the best news I've heard in weeks, no, months!" She sounded elated. "I'm going to call Brad and then, I'll call Jillian and tell her the good news."

When Faith arrived back at the house that evening she phoned Laura.

"Wonderful news! It worked. And it's finally over for me and for Oliver. I wish you could have been there!"

"I couldn't be happier for you! And how I wish I could have been there too. But I knew how important your timing in all this was. I wasn't about to take a chance on slowing you down."

Amazingly, the local media covered the story on the six o'clock news that evening. They had been well represented throughout the trial and were quick to report any damage to Oliver. To their credit, they now vindicated him and referred to it as a *true Perry Mason* turn of events. Jason Mabry became an overnight media star.

Less than thirty minutes later, the Allen's phone started ringing from well-wishers calling to offer their congratulations. Some of those who called were folks who had deserted them when the charges were filed. Several confessed that they had "known Oliver was innocent from the onset." *An interesting study in human nature*, Faith mused, as she listened to each of them.

Later that evening, Faith was on such a call when she heard a call-waiting beep. Her first thought was to ignore it, but she decided to answer it. She excused herself for a moment.

"Hello."

"Faith. It's Marcus. I just got off the phone with Laura. I had to call you."

"I'm so glad you did!" Then Faith did something quite out of character. She never even returned to the other caller to say goodbye.

When the trial wrapped up, John Merrill and Scott Hansen were found guilty. Each was sentenced to fifteen years with possibility of parole after seven years and eight months. Henry and Fran Thompson were arrested and would stand trial at some future date.

Oliver and Steven Taylor had been partners for eighteen years when the company was known as Hargrave and Taylor. They had made the decision to bring Henry into the company as a full partner seven years ago. Apparently, Henry had simply become too ambitious. He had wanted to begin with a lifestyle that had taken Oliver and Steven years to attain. His expenditures had far exceeded his earnings and, at first, he told himself he was merely borrowing. But, as time passed, he found himself unable to get his 'loans' paid off, and Oliver was becoming so ill, he had devised this elaborate scheme. Henry had promised Scott Hansen and John Merrill handsome rewards if they would testify against Oliver and not implicate him. He felt they could convince the jury that Oliver was the lone guilty party, and they merely his pawns. They probably would have pulled it off, had it not been for John Merrill's testimony. Faith had no idea why he had wavered on the stand as he did, but she would be eternally grateful to him for doing so. She shuddered to think what would have happened if Fran hadn't lost that earring, and Oliver hadn't found it and died with it still in his possession.

CHAPTER 34

Faith packed all of her belongings and left for the beach the following Wednesday. She had taken the previous weekend to relax and spend time with the boys. She looked forward to getting home again, to having some degree of normalcy in her life, although she wasn't exactly sure anymore just what that would be for her.

She arrived at the beach a little before noon. The day had been overcast during most of the drive down but, as she neared North Myrtle Beach, the sun peered out from the clouds, and by the time she turned into her private drive it was shining brightly. She took it as an omen. Life could only get better!

She had promised herself she would take the rest of the week to do just as she pleased. She would sleep late and walk on the beach. She'd be a true beach bum for the next several days.

Then she would have to get busy. Her finances had taken a terrible hit during the last year, actually the last year and a half. There had been heavy expenses above the insurance coverage as Oliver's condition worsened. In the fourteen months since his death, she had lost money on her Winston-Salem business and on the Cayman Shores house, and her attorney's fees had been staggering. But it had all been worth it to her. She had kept Oliver as comfortable as possible during his last days, and she had publicly cleared him of any wrongdoing. And, in the process, she was beginning to heal. Perhaps now she could start to move forward with her life, as Oliver had wanted her to. She and Jillian had even made a baby step toward friendship. She felt positive about that, and she knew Oliver would also be pleased.

She relayed every word of the testimony during that last afternoon to Laura on Wednesday evening as they walked. By the time they returned to Laura's porch, Faith had to sit down to catch her breath.

"I don't think I've ever seen you this animated and talkative," Laura said, laughing. "It suits you. And I don't blame you. You've been through hell for quite a while now. It's time things went your way."

Laura's phone rang, and she stepped inside to answer it. She reappeared a moment later smiling. "It's for you," she said, holding the receiver out to Faith.

Looking quizzical, Faith put the receiver to her ear, said hello then listened. A smile crossed her lips and she nodded. "It is," she said. "It's wonderful to be home again."

Laura left the porch and went into the kitchen. She returned a few minutes later with a pitcher of lemonade. Faith was off the phone by then.

"So, what did my little brother have to say for himself?" She asked, eyeing Faith.

"He's coming Friday. He's going to spend the weekend."

Laura studied her friend's face for a moment. "Why so serious all of a sudden?"

"I don't know. Marcus said he needs to talk to me. He said he has something serious that he wants to talk to me about." She took a sip of the lemonade Laura had poured for her. All of the exuberance she'd felt earlier seemed to have vanished. An hour later, Faith left to go home. She had no way of knowing that as soon as she left, Laura went to the phone and called her brother.

As Faith lay in bed, she thought of her conversation with Marcus earlier in the evening. She had been so pleased to hear his voice, so happy to hear that he was coming to the shore this weekend, until he had said he wanted to have a serious talk with her. What did he want to talk about? Was she really ready to hear what he wanted to say?

"A serious talk," had instantly made her feel uneasy, a little nervous, and she wasn't sure why. She cared about Marcus, she was coming to realize that. But she had been through a very difficult time and didn't want to have any other complications or decisions to make in her life, at least for a while.

Perhaps he was ready to share with her what had troubled him these last months, this life altering decision he was making so painstakingly. Laura had told her that Marcus would talk to her when he felt the time was right. He had listened to all of her problems whenever she needed to talk. Why was she so reticent to have him talk about his, if that was what he had in mind? Maybe it was that she feared it would somehow change things between them. Was he beginning to care for her? She thought he might be. She didn't know if she was ready for that yet. And she in no way wanted to influence the decision he would come to about his present situation.

As she lay there, she could see his face with her mind's eye. That square jaw that gave him the look of quiet strength. And those wonderful deep blue eyes that appeared so pensive much of the time. In July, when she had last seen him, his skin had taken on a rich golden tan; his sandy hair had been streaked with gold, bleached by the scorching ocean sun.

As she thought of him now, she pictured him on the cover of a paperback novel holding the heroine in his arms. As her thoughts continued, she saw herself as that heroine for one fleeting moment before she sat erect in her bed and whispered, "No! Stop!" She buried her face in her pillow. A pang of guilt shot through her for many reasons: disloyalty to Oliver, and questions about Marcus' other relationship, for starters.

She dreamed of Marcus that night, and when she awakened, as the sun was rising, her thoughts of him began once again. *What's happening to me?* She wondered. *Am I falling...?* She interrupted her own thought. She knew nothing of the man save the tiny glimpses he allowed her on occasion. Otherwise he was a complete mystery to her. She didn't even know how he earned his living. *Is he still married? The first time he visited Laura said he had a large family: that was all, no elaboration, nothing more. And she said he was grappling with a problem.* Laura had been no help in that department either. Faith felt that Laura knew all about it, everything that troubled Marcus, yet she had made it absolutely clear, on more than one occasion, that she would say nothing about it. That Marcus would talk to Faith when he was ready. That seemed to be end of chapter and of book, as far as Laura was concerned.

Faith had to admit that this trait in Laura, though frustrating when it came to Marcus, was one she admired. It made her feel secure in anything that she confided to her friend.

And now was Marcus at last going to entrust her with his secret? For as many times as she had wondered about it, she now felt discomforted when the moment seemed to be close at hand.

She got out of bed and went into the kitchen. She turned on the coffee maker and stuck a slice of bread into the toaster oven, then stepped through the foyer and opened the front door. She walked around the deck to the stairs and picked up her morning newspaper.

She glanced through it as she sipped her coffee and ate her toast. Her eyes struck the headline of a short article toward the back of the business section. It was a summary of the Winston-Salem trial. So that had made it to the beach, too. It concluded with a statement from Steven Taylor. "I'm not sure as to what our future plans are. Right now we're examining several options."

Poor Steven! How thoughtless of her to have run off reveling in her personal victory, completely ignoring the company that Oliver had worked so hard to build; and

Steven Taylor, a loyal friend and associate who had helped him and who now needed loyalty in return. He had called her several times before and during the trial to say how badly he felt at having Oliver dragged into this. She knew he was sincere. And Steven had been so pleased to see Oliver cleared. He had thrown his arms about her as soon as the trial ended.

She and the girls were majority stockholders and, along with Steven's twenty percent, they controlled seventy-one percent of the stock of the company. They must join together to salvage the company for the remaining employees and stockholders.

She picked up the receiver and dialed Steven. They talked for twenty minutes. When they hung up, Faith had agreed to go to Winston-Salem on Tuesday to meet with him. Before she returned to the beach they would call a board meeting.

Marcus arrived late Friday afternoon. He had flown into Wilmington early that morning and rented a car. After spending a couple of hours with the Dixons, he had driven on to North Myrtle Beach. Laura invited Faith to have dinner with them. Laura seemed her happiest when she was in the kitchen with friends and family to cook for. And she didn't mind trying out new recipes. Tonight she had decided on a curried-pork with orange-rind marmalade and wild-rice stuffing recipe she had found in a magazine.

Faith felt a little apprehensive as she knocked on the porch door at the Halls'. Laura let her in and, as they walked back to the kitchen, there was no sign of Marcus. She glanced out the kitchen window, wondering if he was working on his boat.

Laura must have noticed because she said, "He's not out there. He went in to take a shower. Should be out any minute now."

"How did he find your aunt and uncle? Well, I hope."

"Marcus and I really haven't had much time to talk. He hasn't been here long, but I guess they've been busy. I've been trying to get them down for a few days, but Uncle Charles has been too absorbed in church affairs to leave. I guess that's good; his church is growing. It seems that hard work really does pay off."

"Yes, it does," Marcus said, as he stepped from the hall into the kitchen.

Faith felt her face flush. "Hi." She smiled at him.

He smiled back, stepped over to her and embraced her. She felt her pulse quicken as her arms encircled his broad shoulders for a long moment.

He released her. "I'm taking drink orders," he said, stepping over to the wet bar. "It's been a hot one today. How does a Margarita sound?"

"That always hits the spot with me," Laura told him.

The minute she had laid eyes on Marcus, Faith's uneasiness began to fade. It felt right to have him here, with them, and she never failed to seem a little empty when he left. She realized it now, or had she known for some time and only now allowed herself to acknowledge the fact?

The recipe Laura tried had been spicy but delicious and very filling. Throughout the meal, Faith's eyes kept turning toward Marcus. And his eyes always met her gaze.

The three decided to take their customary walk after the kitchen had been tidied. Faith excused herself for a moment and went into the bathroom before they left. As she started back down the hall to rejoin them, she heard Laura's voice.

"Is everything worked out then? Is it finally settled?" she asked.

"Not quite. It's moving more slowly than I thought. It shouldn't be long though. It should just be a matter of days, weeks at most, before I receive the paperwork."

Faith cleared her throat as she rejoined them. "Ready?"

They left the house and started down the beach. "I think I could walk this route with my eyes blindfolded," Laura said. "I believe I could even guess how many steps it is to the pier, give or take fifty." She laughed. "On one of my good days anyway," she added.

As always, they walked to the end of the pier and climbed up to the observation deck to watch the tide begin its journey out to sea and to allow Laura a little time to rest. It was still hot. The day's temperature had been in the high nineties, and the only respite from the intense heat had been the constant wind. Tonight the breeze had died down considerably and as a result the air felt quite muggy. They must have sat there for thirty minutes before Laura suggested they head back.

As usual, Laura stopped off at her place, and Marcus and Faith continued on to Faith's. He left her at her gazebo but watched until she opened the door and waved goodnight. "See you in the morning," she called.

"Until then."

They were going sailing the next day. They planned to leave early, drive to the marina to pick up the sailboat and make a day of it. Faith fully expected that Marcus would take advantage of their time together tomorrow to have that serious talk. She no longer felt quite so uneasy about it; in fact, she was quite curious now after hearing that snippet of conversation between brother and sister.

They set sail by nine o'clock the following morning, and traveled south, down through North and south

Myrtle Beach. Laura had packed some snacks and cold drinks for them, but they planned to dock and eat at one of the restaurants on Pawleys Island.

It was a restful, pleasant day, but their conversation was no different than it had been in the past. Faith decided to ask Marcus about the pilot he said he attended college with. Perhaps that would be a key to opening a door to his past.

"You mentioned knowing the pilot on one of your previous flights. Which college did you attend?"

"UNC. I knew him in undergrad school."

"According to many alumni, we should be bitter enemies. I went to State." She chuckled. "I take it then that you went on to graduate school."

"I did."

"And you studied?"

"I got my doctorate in psychology."

"So, are you in private practice?"

"No. I'd like to be though."

By his brief answers and body language, it was clear that he felt uncomfortable with the subject, so Faith let it drop. She wondered why. She thought back to a previous time when they had sailed together. She recalled him using the phrase, "in a place where nothing corrupt can touch me." She had thought it a strange choice of words. Was that somehow a reference to some sort of professional problem he had encountered? Could he have perhaps lost his license for some reason, scandal of some sort? No. She couldn't believe that of him, not Marcus.

He seemed too honest, too principled. They sailed for sometime without talking at all.

Lunch was delicious. By mid-afternoon, they were headed back toward home. As often happened when she spoke with Marcus, the topic turned to her faith.

"After all of those months that I felt I had either a one-way conversation or no communication at all with God, I can feel my faith returning," she confessed. "I felt so isolated, actually betrayed by Him. Recently, I've realized how wrong I was. These new feelings started even before the trial began, when everything was at its darkest. He hadn't deserted me. He just wasn't giving me any of the answers I was pleading, even bargaining, for. I know you can't make deals with God to get what you want. I wasn't thinking clearly for so long. I was acting out of desperation."

He looked at her for a long moment and smiled. "I'm glad to hear you say that. At times, I think we all tend to look at his silence as unanswered prayer, when it isn't that at all. I believe that is when He wants us to accept His silence and use it to our advantage, perhaps use it as a time for introspection, to search for other choices and alternatives. And in our acceptance, perhaps grow in character"

She was thoughtful for a moment. "I think you're exactly right." Perhaps that was what Marcus had done, and now he had made the decision he'd been struggling with. he thought he was about to tell her when approaching boats distracted them.

Three large motor boats pulled along side dangerously along side, causing a series of rough waves that rocked the sailboat violently. One of the passengers laughed as they were along side. He held up a can of beer in a mock toast then tossed the can at them. It would have hit Faith's shoulder had she not ducked.

"Jerk," Marcus shouted, shaking his head.

They didn't return to their previous conversation.

As they neared the marina, Faith determined that Marcus was not going to discuss his situation with her, at least not today.

"I have to leave early tomorrow," he told her on the drive back home.

When they reached her place he went around to her door, opened it and offered her his hand. "Go to dinner with me tonight? he asked his hand still wrapped about hers.

"What time?" She smiled up at him.

"I'll come for you at eight."

"I'll be ready."

He looked marvelous that evening as he stood at her door wearing white Dockers and a Carolina Blue golf shirt that matched his eyes. The wind was gently blowing his sun streaked hair. Faith felt a warm flush as she held the door open and he stepped in so close to her that their bodies brushed slightly.

"You look beautiful tonight, Faith." She thought his voice sounded a little husky. She found it very sensuous.

"Thanks." She smiled. "You're not bad to look at yourself." After she said it, she felt slightly embarrassed.

She wondered if it had sounded too flirtatious. Had she rolled her eyes at him?

She'd dressed in a cream-colored, sleeveless sheath. The back of the dress was open and dipped a third of the way down her back and had two straps that criss-crossed over her bare skin.

He chucked, apparently pleased. "That's a good color for you," he said, nodding his head. "It almost matches your hair. It's good with your tan, too."

She thought it made her eyes look bluer. She had noticed that as soon as she put it on. "I'm ready if you are," she said. "Unless you'd like a drink before we go."

"No thanks. I never drink when I drive."

He took her to J. Edwards. "It's a family favorite," he told her, as they pulled into the parking lot.

"One of mine, too," she agreed.

The meal was excellent, as was usual for that restaurant. They arrived back at Faith's place at ten-thirty.

"Let's walk a little," Marcus said." "I'm not ready for this evening to end."

Faith fell into step with him. They walked the opposite direction that they went with Laura. They didn't talk much, just walked, but it felt so comfortable to Faith. Marcus made her feel secure, she found herself comparing this evening to time spent with Oliver.

At last they returned to her cottage. They walked up the stairs slowly and on along the pier to the gazebo where they sat side by side. They were mostly silent, watching the pattern of the waves as the tide washed out to sea and the moon cast shadows of the gazebo on the sand beneath them.

Finally, Marcus rose and reached out to her.

She took his hand and stood.

"As much as I hate for this evening to end, I need to be on the road at five-thirty in the morning."

They walked to her door. She found the key in her purse, stuck it into the lock and opened it.

Marcus looked down into her eyes, "Let's not say good-bye, just goodnight," he said softly.

Then, before she even realized what was happening, he wrapped his arms about her and drew her to him. His lips pressed against hers. She leaned into him and returned his kiss. As he drew her even tighter to him, she could feel his body tremble slightly.

"Faith," he whispered. He kissed her hungrily as she melted against him. Her head was spinning, she hadn't felt these sensations in such a long time. She wanted to cry from the pure joy of being able to feel the emotion again.

Suddenly he straightened and held her back at arm's length.

"Not yet. I'm sorry, Faith. Forgive me."

He turned and left her at her door bewildered and shaken, not understanding what had just happened.

CHAPTER 35

On Tuesday, Faith packed a bag and headed for Winston-Salem to meet with Steven Taylor as promised. As she drove, she thought of Marcus. In fact, she had thought of him much of the time since he had left her Saturday evening.

Upon entering the house that evening, she had gone into her bedroom and removed Oliver's letter from her dresser drawer. She took it out of the envelope and read, this time only the last page; his wish for her to go on for both of them. And he had given her permission. No. He had encouraged her to find happiness again, without him. For the first time since she lost Oliver, Faith began to think it might be possible.

Marcus had stirred feeling in her that had been dormant for a very long time. She knew he cared for her. They had been friends for a long time now, and he had never kissed her until tonight; though once before she thought he had wanted to. There had been such hunger in his kisses, she had felt his body tremble as he drew her near. True, he had been the one to break away but he had said, "Not yet." And he had told her that he hated to leave her.

For all she didn't know about Marcus, there was one thing about him that was very clear. He didn't take commitments lightly or walk away from them easily. She knew he had given this much thought. And she also knew in her heart that he would come back to her when he was free to do so.

When she reached Winston-Salem, she drove out Country Club Road to Taylor-Hargrave as the firm was now called, at her insistence; Steven Taylor was waiting for her. She went into his office and he closed the door with orders that they not be interrupted.

Steven had pulled some of the company's financial records together in a folder for Faith to follow along as he talked her through their situation. They began with the company's balance sheet, starting with a look at the real estate.

The building that currently housed the operation was valued at five and a quarter million dollars and there was no mortgage against it. However, real estate sales had slowed over the past six months, so it might not bring that amount on the open market. They owned one other building, the one they had purchased when the company was three years old and looking very promising. When they outgrew it, they sectioned it off and now rented it out to several small businesses. It brought in approximately eight thousand dollars in rent each month.

They had lost a number of accounts when the scandal hit the papers, but they had also retained many loyal and satisfied customers. Steven told Faith that so far three accounts that had left were in various stages of returning, and he felt confident that they would once the numbers were worked out.

Then there was the matter of the company stock. It was currently selling for twenty-one dollars a share, an all time low since the company's inception. Steven had been talking with VanCampen-Zemeckus, a large firm from Richmond, Virginia, about the possibility of a merger. They were big into the pharmaceutical and optical advertising market. If that merger took place, it would give the new company much greater diversity than either of them had separately. The executives of the other company had also said they'd do their best, if we do consolidate, to see that none of Taylor-Hargrave's one hundred fifty-five employees would lose their jobs.

"Right now, it's a real challenge to meet our payroll, and I've been honest about that fact with VanCampen-Zemeckus. The cash they would initially pour into our operation would be a Godsend, and the merger would also boost the price of the stock considerably," Steven concluded.

"It sounds as if you've thought this out very clearly. Do you trust them when they say that they'll keep on all of the employees who want to stay?"

"I hope they're being honest with me on that point. Often those promises aren't kept, but I don't see that we have much choice in the matter. We need to do something to get back on our feet."

"It sounds like this is a logical answer to all of the current problems. You've been busy. I think Oliver would be pleased. I think he'd do exactly as you're doing if he were in your shoes."

"Thanks for your confidence, Faith. It means a great deal to me." He reached for her hand and gave it a little squeeze. "I know all of this has been terribly rough on you. I know that you've had to close your business down. I'm sorry that happened. You worked hard to build it, and you're a top-notch decorator. No one would argue that point."

"I thought it best, all things considered. Linda is opening up her own shop. But thanks, I appreciate that. I guess I was a just a casualty of the war."

"What I'm getting at, is that I'd like to offer you a position in our finance department. You have a good head for business. We could use your talent, if you'd consider moving back to the area."

"You don't know how much that means to me, Steven. But I really don't want to leave the beach now. I've gotten back into decorating again. I've done a couple of projects and have several more in the works. Thanks for your offer."

"Well, I'm happy for you. I know it's your first love. And, I appreciate your concern for the company. It was good of you to want to come today."

"Is it premature to call a board meeting?"

"No. I think it's called for. Since most of our shareholders are in the immediate area, I think we can set it for Thursday. That way you can get back to your beloved beach by the weekend. Anyway, they'll do what we think is best, because we control the majority of the stock," he said with a smile and a wink.

The board meeting was a mere formality. Everyone agreed that the merger was the healthiest solution for the troubled company. Steven Taylor was given a vote of approval to proceed on that course.

At the conclusion of the meeting, when they were the only two remaining in the boardroom, Faith told Steven that she had great faith in him and his abilities. She assured him whatever he felt was best for the company; he could count on her support.

Faith left Mary Jane and Brad's Saturday morning and headed home. She stopped by the grocery store on the way into town and was home by early afternoon. She put up the groceries and made herself a sandwich, then she changed into shorts and went out to the beach.

As she walked, she glanced down toward Laura's and noticed a strange car in the driveway. Could it be a rental? Was Marcus back? Her pulse quickened. As she neared their place, she saw a man sitting in a beach chair on the shore surf fishing. It was Ben Hall! She had no idea that they had planned to visit.

"Hello," she called as she got within earshot of him. The wind was so noisy that he didn't hear her. She stepped closer and touched his shoulder lightly. "Hello, Ben!"

He turned his weather-beaten face to look up at her, and grinned. "Well, Faith. Come over here and give me a squeeze," he said rising. "You're a sight for sore old eyes. How are you?"

"I'm doing better, much better thanks in part to your family."

"You're a big topic of conversation with Laura these days. She thinks the world of you!"

"The feeling's mutual."

"Listen. Kitty and I were just sick to hear about Oliver. You should have let us know. I had no idea of the seriousness of his condition. I'm so very sorry, I wish we had known." He was silent for a moment.

"I was just so…" She shook her head.

"I know. I understand," he said, gently patting her shoulder. "Laura and her mom went shopping. Heaven knows when they'll be back. Kitty's a real pro, so it could be hours. Why don't you sit down here and keep me company? Maybe we'll catch us all some dinner."

She kicked off her sandals and sat down on the sand beside his chair. They visited about Ben and Kitty's travels. They had gone to Europe after Kitty's trip to Hawaii. Ben had been doing some consulting for an engineering firm since they returned. When he finished his commitment, they took advantage of the leisure time to come to the beach.

"I've really enjoyed spending a little time with your sister Jean and her husband, Charles."

"Hmmm," he grunted. His body stiffened a bit, and he changed the subject abruptly. "Say, it's gettin' a might thirsty out here. You don't suppose I could impose on you to go in and get me a cold beer, do you?"

"I'll be glad to, I know my way around your kitchen," she smiled at him.

"Bring along a chair when you come back, if you like."

She left and returned a few minutes later with his beer. "What, no chair?" he asked.

"I love sitting on the sand."

"Didn't you want anything?" he asked as he took the bottle from her and twisted the cap off.

"No, thanks. I drank a glass of water while I was inside."

They chatted for a few more minutes and Marcus's name came up. "He's been such a help to me through all of this," Faith told Ben. "He listened to my problems. I felt I could tell him most anything. He's very special."

"Special? You bet he is. He's damn special!" His face took on the glow of pride. "And, that's what he's trained to do. That's what priests do, and Marcus is a damn good priest."

Faith suppressed a gasp. She felt the color drain from her face. She stared at Ben in stunned silence.

CHAPTER 36

He's a priest! He's a priest. Ben's revelation spun in her
head, and she couldn't remember anything else he had
said. Faith was still in shock when she reached her home.
For some time, she wasn't sure how long, she had stayed
after Ben dropped that bombshell. She thought, at least
she hoped, her manner hadn't betrayed her inner anguish.

The women were still out shopping when she left
him. She had told Ben that her head was aching, and
she wanted to go home and rest. It wasn't a lie! Her
head began throbbing almost the moment those words
left Ben's mouth.

She had left Ben Hall…and then, she was at home.
She hadn't been aware of walking there. She was just in
her living room, and then she was in the bedroom. She
sank onto the bed and buried her face in her pillow, but
there were no tears, just hurt… and anger.

How could he? How could Marcus do this to her? She had allowed herself to trust him. She had trusted Fran and Henry Thompson, and they had let her down, too. Marcus had seemed so wonderful, so charming, but he had no right. She thought she was beginning to fall in love with him. To fall in love with a Roman Catholic priest! She had been so fragile for such a long time. And she had thought she could never love again. But slowly she had begun to trust Marcus. The caring for him had crept up on her. Surely he could see that she was beginning to have feelings for him, and he knew it was forbidden. Why had he put her in that position? That he hadn't confided in her, she found unforgivable.

She rolled over onto her back and shook her head. Thoughts continued to race through her mind. He hadn't really led her on. But why hadn't he told her right from the start that he was a priest? Why be so secretive?

Perhaps she was misreading him. Perhaps this romantic thing was all in *her* head. He had never made a romantic move toward her… until that last night. Up until then, all he had ever professed to be was her friend and confidant. No wonder she felt so comfortable with him. And, had she known that he was a priest, would she have been able to confide in him about her feeling toward God as she had? About her deepest, and sometimes, very darkest feelings? She wasn't sure she could have been as open with him. Getting it all out, as he let her, had helped her begin to recover her peace of mind and, with it, understanding. She was regaining her lost faith because of it.

She had truly needed what he was able to give her. He had helped her begin to heal herself. But that last night there was no mistaking his feelings. He had kissed her with such desire.

Then there was her "dear friend" Laura. She had known all along, and she never even gave a hint as to what troubled him. She and Laura had grown so close, and she thought Laura knew she was beginning to care for Marcus. She felt angry with Laura. Laura should have said something to warn her.

Faith rose from her bed and went out to the kitchen to get a cold drink. While she was there, her phone rang. She didn't answer it. She had no intention of talking to anyone tonight. She poured herself a Coke and took it out to the gazebo.

She couldn't turn her mind off. She knew Laura wasn't one to discuss anyone else's business, but *this* was different. Faith felt betrayed. Laura should have at least told her that Marcus was a priest. She should have confided that much of his business to her. She thought she heard her phone ring again. She didn't make a move to go inside. She was afraid it might be Laura, and she didn't want to talk to her or any of them for now.

Tuesday evening there was a knock on Faith's door. When she opened it a crack, she saw Laura holding a covered pie tin in her hands.

"Mom and Dad left this afternoon," she said. "May I come in and talk?"

Faith hesitated for a moment.

"Please. Let me come in." Her eyes were imploring.

Faith opened the door wider and stood aside.

"I come bearing humble pie," she said soberly, offering Faith the pie.

Faith noticed that Laura was limping tonight. Perhaps her stress had caused a flair-up. "Thank you," she said stiffly. She took the pie from Laura and carried it to the kitchen table. Laura didn't follow her as she ordinarily would have.

When Faith rejoined her, she began haltingly, "I know… I know my dad told you…about Marcus, I mean. Faith, I'm so sorry you had to hear it that way. I feel that I'm to blame." Tears brimmed in Laura's eyes as she spoke, and, as she stood looking at Faith, they began to roll down her cheeks.

Laura looked so sad that it touched Faith's heart. She stepped toward Laura and put her arms around her.

"I hope you can understand what a terrible shock all this has been to me. I feel either Marcus or you should have told me. It shouldn't have had to come from Ben." She released Laura.

"That's why it's my fault." Laura dabbed at her tears. "Marcus wanted to tell you himself. He planned to when he came down this last time. But that night, when you got back from the trial, you were so elated. Marcus had called your home and when he got no answer, he reached you at my place. You said he told you that he wanted to have a serious talk with you and, suddenly, you became so solemn. I worried that his timing was wrong. When you left, I phoned him and told him not to rush things. I thought you needed time to recover from the trial, time with no complications or decisions to make. You'd been through so much. And I'm so sorry. I shouldn't have interfered. I don't usually. And when I didn't hear anything from you these last three days, and you wouldn't answer your phone, I knew you were really angry with me."

"I won't lie to you. I am. Because I think you've known that Marcus was becoming very important to me; and you let that continue. You should have told me! I feel," she paused as she searched for the right words, "at the very least, deeply hurt."

Laura had been shifting her weight from one foot to the other. Now she blotted her eyes with the tissue she had been twisting between her fingers. She sat down in one of the living room chairs.

"If Marcus hadn't come to this decision, if he had resolved this conflict and felt that he should remain a priest, then he felt that the fewer people who knew, the better. When he came here to the beach, it was to reflect; he was just Marcus Hall. That was the way he wanted it. And I want you to understand, Faith, his decision has been made. All the details aren't completed yet, but Marcus will talk to you about that. And you had nothing to do with it; his frustration and indecision began long before you were ever in the picture.

"I'm worried about Dad, though, and I'm worried about Marcus and Dad's relationship. Dad's angry with Uncle Charles and Aunt Jean, too. And that isn't like our family. We've never quarreled before. Dad doesn't know it's final yet, and I don't know how he's going to accept this when Marcus tells him. I worry about him." She shook her head dejectedly. "At first he was angry when the topic was broached, but lately I think he's put blinders on. He was so proud when Marcus was ordained. It was a lifelong dream of our father. And now he so desperately wants to believe that Marcus is fulfilled in the priesthood that I think he's in denial."

Faith was thoughtful for quite a while. Laura sat patiently, wiping her eyes occasionally.

Finally, Faith spoke. "I have a little better understanding of the situation now.

And I'm grateful for what you told me tonight. I know it wasn't easy coming here feeling that I was angry with you. And, I know you feel that the rest of the explanation is between Marcus and me. But I do have one other question, and I feel I need an answer from you. and, I must admit that this totally threw me off."

"What's that?"

"That first time when Marcus was here and Grant was down. They hit it off so well, Marcus had such amazing rapport with him. I asked if he had a family, and you said he had a large one. I thought that he was in an unhappy marriage and was struggling with the decision of whether to leave it."

Laura looked into Faith's eyes. "Don't you see? He was. Being a priest *is* like a marriage to him. And he does have a large family. Only not like you and I would have. He has always felt that each parish becomes his family for as long as he is with them."

Faith was thoughtful for a moment. "Well, I understand what you meant, but it was terribly misleading."

Laura nodded, "I guess it was if you aren't used to thinking that way. Maybe we should have had this talk sooner. At least I'm glad we had it tonight. I love you, Faith. I don't want to lose you as my friend, but I love my brother, too." She gave Faith a rather poignant smile.

"Me, too," Faith said, "You're one of God's best, Laura. True friendships survive misunderstandings. Even ones as big as this."

Laura looked somewhat relieved. "I guess a good share of life's problems arise from explanations that aren't clear or come too late. Sometimes an omission can be just as disastrous as a lie. I was torn between you and Marcus. I really am sorry, Faith."

Laura stayed on for another half-hour before returning home. Though their discussion had shed much more light on the situation, Faith still felt very uneasy about it.

Before she left, Faith had asked Laura if Marcus was aware of the conversation between Ben and her. Laura said she had called him to tell him about it earlier this evening.

Faith lifted the receiver to call Marcus and realized she didn't have a number for him. In fact, he had always been the one to contact her. She didn't know what she would say to him if she did reach him, but she felt quite sure that Laura would talk to him as soon as she returned home to fill him in on their conversation. And that was fine with her. It would undoubtedly make things easier when they did talk. Perhaps he would call her later. Her phone didn't ring all evening.

By the following evening she hadn't heard from Marcus, and she hadn't spoken with Laura either. She felt restless and unsettled. She wanted to speak with Laura, but she didn't want to. She wanted to hear from Marcus, but she had a feeling that he wasn't going to call her. She turned on the TV but paid no attention to it. She straightened one of the pictures on the wall then rearranged the magazines on the lower shelf of the coffee table.

"This is ridiculous," she finally said aloud. She reached for the receiver and dialed Laura's number.

"I want to call Marcus," she said quietly.

"I think that would be good," Laura replied. Faith jotted his number down.

They hung up shortly after. Faith paced the floor for a few minutes trying to gather her thoughts. She still wasn't sure what she was going to say as she began to dial the number. Her stomach churned as she counted four rings. She was about to hang up, when, to her surprise, a female voice answered.

CHAPTER 37

It was the housekeeper. Faith waited a moment, then a male came on the line.

"Marcus?" she asked uncertainly. The voice sounded strained, yet familiar.

"Yes. Faith, is that you?"

"It is." There was an awkward silence. "I, I felt we needed to talk," she finally managed.

"I know. I was going to call you later tonight. I should have told you myself, and I think it would be better if we talk in person. Laura's flying up this weekend, Friday afternoon. I think she said her plane gets in at five. Would you please come with her?"

"This weekend? She didn't mention it." "I know. She was leaving that to me."

"I don't even know if I could get a ticket this late."

"She has one for you, if you'll come."

"I...I don't know what to say."

"Say yes," he said softly.

Faith was silent.

CHAPTER 38

It rained during the morning Friday but stopped around noon. It was chilly and overcast as the plane took off for Philadelphia. Faith was relieved. She hated to fly in a storm. Marcus planned to meet them at the airport. Laura told her that Marcus had asked their parents to come, too. Ben and Kitty planned to fly in on Saturday afternoon.

It was a smooth flight, and the plane arrived on time and to much nicer weather than they had left behind. As the pilot announced their approach to Philadelphia International Airport, Faith felt the butterflies beginning to stir in her stomach. Would it be awkward? Would their conversation be strained? She was glad Laura was there. She would be somewhat of a buffer for both of them. She wondered if Marcus was having some of the same feelings she was.

They were two of the last to exit the plane. Though she was walking well today, Laura still wanted to let the crowd disperse before she started up the ramp. "I want to be able to take my time and not hold anyone up," she said.

Marcus was waiting for them as they entered the US Air gate fifty-seven arrival area. He wore a sports coat and turtleneck as Oliver so often had. Faith couldn't help but reflect that she had never seen him in a clerical collar. And no one seeing him today would ever take him for a Catholic priest.

Laura stepped ahead of Faith and greeted her brother with a hug. Faith lingered behind. They turned back to her, and for a brief moment they all looked at one another. Faith thought Marcus looked like a little boy uncertain of what he should do next, and Laura wore a somber expression.

Suddenly Faith extended her arms to him. He stepped toward her and embraced her.

"I was so afraid you wouldn't come," he whispered into her ear.

A little shiver went through her and, as they parted, she noticed some of the tension had left Laura's face. Moments later, they picked up their luggage and went out to Marcus' car.

"Your reservations are at the Foxwood Suites," he told them as they drove.

They reached the motel a little before six and checked in. Marcus went with them to their second story suite. It was attractively appointed in burgundy, mauve and green, they even had a fireplace, though they wouldn't need it tonight as the temperature was unseasonably warm. The suite had a kitchenette and two bedrooms, each with an adjoining bathroom.

"Mom and Dad will be just a couple doors down from you," Marcus said as he put their luggage down. "I thought we'd go out for dinner once you're settled."

"If you don't mind," Laura said, "I'd like to rest for a little while first. Why don't you keep Faith company, Marcus?"

"I can do that," he smiled at his sister.

Faith had the feeling that this had been pre-arranged, but she wasn't upset with them. She and Marcus needed some time to talk. She suspected that he felt as uncomfortable as she did. Laura left them and went into one of the bedrooms.

"So, how was the flight?" Marcus asked once they were alone.

"Very good," she told him, smiling.

"I'm sorry. I know we've already had this conversation. I guess I'm just...I'm trying to find the right words to explain this debacle I seem to have put us in, to give you some insight as to what I've been feeling for such a long time and why I kept it from almost everyone until now."

Faith nodded at him. "I know. I'm a little uncomfortable, too." Somehow, saying the words out loud seemed to relieve some of her tension. She noticed that Marcus also appeared to relax a bit.

251

"Faith, I know I should have been more open with you from the beginning. But when I first met you, you were in such pain. You certainly didn't need to have anyone else's problems unloaded on you."

Ever so gently, he took her arm and guided her out onto the balcony. He pulled the door shut behind them. "I've been struggling with this for years. It started long before I ever met you." He paused and looked her in the eyes. "You had nothing whatsoever to do with the inner turmoil I've been trying to resolve."

"I do remember that the first time I met you, you were so in tune with Grant that day, and yet that evening when we stayed for dinner, you seemed to be entirely remote from us. It was almost as if you were in another place altogether."

He nodded, "I know. That was a particularly difficult time. I was beginning to admit to myself what the crux of my whole problem was. That was why I went to the coast at that time, to clear my head, get the garbage out and try to address the real issue.

"As a child, I used to speak of wanting to be a priest. I think lots of little boys go through a stage when the priesthood looks appealing, just as little girls talk of becoming nuns. But I remember how proud and pleased my father was whenever I talked about it. And that was so important to me. I guess it's his Irish ancestry. Anyway, Dad was a top-notch engineer, with large companies all over the East Coast vying for his services. Dad was a hero to me, a great man, and having his approval meant everything to me.

"But, when I went to college, Psychology was what I wanted to study. I got my doctorate. Still, Dad kept reminding me of "my" childhood dream and what a tool my psychology would be to bring with me to the priesthood.

"I entered the seminary. I'll have to admit that I was happy, for a while. I felt fulfilled, that I could make a difference. The day I was ordained, I think my father was about the happiest I had ever seen him. This super-successful man had tears of pride in his eyes for me. I had earned his complete and total respect. I can't tell you how that made me feel."

"I think we all want to live up to our parents expectations for us. That's very natural."

"I agree."

"But we have to be true to ourselves first. It wasn't long before I began to feel discontented and out of place. Then, I became so angry with myself for having those feelings. I began to feel as if I were being torn apart. I searched my soul, and there were days that I wondered if I even had one any longer. I prayed Lord, what do you want of me? And, why can't I be fulfilled in serving you in this way any longer? I tried to listen, but I couldn't hear any answers. I felt that until I could make my own peace, I would have a hard time counseling others in finding theirs. The words I articulated to them sounded empty to me. I could be in a cathedral filled to capacity and feel totally alone.

"I finally spoke about my doubts with Father Michael, my superior here at Blessed Mother, and I asked for counseling. I, a doctor of Psychology, couldn't heal myself. I counseled with my Bishop. I broached the topic with my father on several occasions. They always ended disastrously. I turned to my Uncle Charles as a man of the cloth and a member of my family. And, as you are aware, I talked with Laura a great deal. They each, in their own way with the exception of Dad, helped me get to the root of my discontent. Slowly, I felt myself coming together again, but only after I began to consider the possibility of leaving the priesthood. I started to feel that I was hearing some answers to all of the questions I had asked of God before. And that's why I said to you, that day at sea, that sometimes we take His silence as unanswered prayer when it isn't at all. He is silently sending us the tools we need to work it all out."

Faith nodded her head slowly as she listened to him without interruption.

"When I was in college, I dated. I liked women. But I never found anyone that I was in love with, anyone I wanted to spend the rest of my life with. And I guess I thought, possibly because of that, that I could become a priest and spend my life in celibacy. But I can't. I can't live that way any longer. And I won't be dishonest about it.

I won't live a life in the shadows either. I knew that, even before I met you. I knew that I wanted to be married to the right woman, maybe even have children.

"I've seen some priests along the way who have broken their vows and continued on as if they hadn't. If it works for them, so be it; it isn't for me to judge.

But, that isn't my way." He was silent for a moment as if he were gathering his thoughts to go on.

Faith said nothing, but tears glistened in her eyes. She could completely understand his feelings as he had recounted them to her. What if she had had to spend a whole lifetime working at something she felt lost in, without ever loving anyone the way she had loved Oliver? She didn't think she could have done it either. What a high price a priest must be willing to pay when he is called. She respected Marcus for recognizing that he couldn't do what was asked of him, for being willing to walk away rather than dishonor his vows.

He broke the silence. "I invited you to come here this weekend because this is the last Sunday that I'll be presiding over the Mass as a priest. I wanted the people I love to be here with me for that. And I need to talk to my parents as I've talked with you. I want to tell my father in person, before Sunday, to try to make him understand that this is his dream for me, not mine...that I didn't have a true calling. I need for him to accept that I went into the priesthood for the wrong reasons, that you don't ever make that kind of commitment to please someone else. It has to be for your reasons. If it isn't, you cheat God, as well as yourself. I won't do that. I'll serve Him in another way."

As Faith looked up into Marcus' blue eyes, she was filled with mixed emotions.

CHAPTER 39

Saturday morning, Faith awakened to the shrill ringing of the phone. She lifted the receiver to answer it and heard Laura's voice and conversation. She hung up and checked the bedside clock. It was nine-thirty, she got out of bed.

By the time she showered, dressed and went out into the living room, Laura had the coffee brewing. "That was Mom. She said the weather in Richmond is awful. They're under a tornado watch. The planes are grounded for now. Dad says if they can't book a flight later in the day, and if the weather clears enough, that they'll drive up."

Faith shook her head. "I didn't think this was tornado season, but I guess they can happen anytime. It's scary to think of driving in bad weather, too."

"I hope it clears and they can fly in. If they can't, it'll be bad news for Marcus. He wanted this evening with

Dad, to prepare him. I hate to say this but, if they can't get in here tonight, then I hope they just don't come. Marcus can visit them when he leaves here."

They had stopped by a market on the way back from dinner the evening before to buy some breakfast food. Faith put a couple of English Muffins into the toaster and poured them each a glass of orange juice. When they had finished eating, Faith washed up their few dishes, and they both read for a while. Later in the afternoon, Laura called Marcus.

"Mornin', or I should say afternoon." She was silent for a moment, then said, "Well, I guess that's that." She listened. "Okay. See you in church." She hung up and turned back to Faith.

"Someone took a message for him from Mom. They've left and are driving. They have one stop to make on the way, and she said they'd see us when they get here."

Faith looked at Laura and shrugged. "Nothing we can do about it then."

"I know, but I don't like this. I'm worried. I know our dad. Marcus needs some private time with him, and I'm afraid he's not going to have it."

Marcus hadn't planned to see the women on Saturday. He was finishing his packing and had a number of church-related duties he needed to wrap up. His letter from Rome, releasing him from his vows had arrived the end of the week and, as of Sunday at midnight, he would no longer be a priest. He would move out of his quarters after the ten o'clock Mass.

He had planned to be finished in time to spend the evening with his parents, and, when they changed the plans, he ended up taking Laura and Faith to dinner. He tried to sound upbeat, but Faith could tell that his spirits had been dampened. Laura was quiet, too. It was still early when Marcus dropped them at the motel; he didn't go in. It had been a rather somber evening. As Faith reflected on everything that had transpired recently to bring her to where she was, she wondered what tomorrow would hold for all of them. *Just what did they expect of Ben Hall? Why were they so worried?* The Ben Hall she'd known had been easy-going, congenial, and downright jovial at times. *What did they expect him to do? Certainly he wouldn't do anything disruptive while in the church that he was so devoted to, or would he?*

CHAPTER 40

The pre-arranged limo picked Faith and Laura up at their motel at 9:15 Sunday morning and drove them to Blessed Mother Catholic Church. There had been no word from Ben and Kitty. Laura began to think that her prayers had been answered; that they would arrive after ten o'clock Mass had ended.

"They probably stayed over with friends in Baltimore, and they'll come on in this afternoon."

"Perhaps," Faith agreed hopefully.

Traffic was relatively light, and the drive took only twenty minutes. The church was large and impressive. It reminded Faith of an English cathedral. Inside, it was beautiful, too, with rich mahogany paneling and pews upholstered in plush purple velvet.

The stained-glass windows were exquisite, and the stations-of-the-cross looked to be of imported Italian marble. Faith looked about in awe. What a spectacular place Marcus had had to call home for the last three years. And yet he had told her that he felt lost, out of place. Surroundings don't always make the difference; if there is no harmony within, all the beauty in the world could envelop you and be missed. How well she understood that in those early months after she lost Oliver. Most days, she could have been in Buckingham Palace and never have noticed.

She heard the swell of the pipe organ, and then the choir began to sing. It was almost time for mass to begin when an usher stopped at their pew with Ben and Kitty Hall following behind him. Kitty slid in beside Laura.

Faith felt Laura's vice-like grip on her left wrist. She leaned forward in her seat and nodded at Ben and Kitty as the procession of altar-servers, a deacon and an elderly priest, whom she assumed to be Father Michael, started down the center aisle of the church. Behind him, Father Marcus, handsome and stately in his vestments, approached the altar for the last time as a priest.

CHAPTER 41

As Marcus passed their pew, Faith felt a lump in her throat. She felt moved by the music and the solemn ceremony of all that surrounded her. And she felt fragile, as if she might weep at any moment, for she realized just what this day meant for Marcus, and she felt such empathy for him.

It was the culmination of years of soul searching and introspection. As if that weren't enough, he had the added concern of how his father would react to the decision that Marcus had felt compelled to make. He looked wonderful, almost regal, as he stood at the front of the church in his cream-colored chasuble, white alb and rich green stole, wearing a large silver cross about his neck.

As the congregation rose to sing the opening hymn, Faith stood and opened her hymnal, but she didn't sing. Instead, she closed her eyes and prayed a silent prayer.

Lord, this man has helped me through some of my most difficult times. He helped me to find you again, to have faith in you once more. When I felt you had turned your back on me, he showed me that you hadn't, in his quiet, reflective way. Please help him through this very important day in his life.

She felt moisture welling in her eyes as she became aware that Marcus was asking the congregation to bow their heads in prayer. She obeyed.

She heard the scripture, the homily and the creed. Then Marcus began to prepare for communion. They said the Lord's Prayer and offered their hands in peace to those around them. It all seemed to be drifting around her in an almost dreamlike sequence. And then the usher was standing at the end of their pew; Faith rose and stepped into the aisle and followed the procession of people until she stood before Marcus.

As he placed the host in her hands, she saw moisture in his eyes. She paused for a moment, then crossed herself and turned to leave. Tears stung in her eyes and blurred her vision. By the time she reached her seat, her cheeks were wet. She fumbled in her handbag for a tissue and became aware of someone holding something white out to her. She looked up and saw that it was Ben. He was passing her his linen handkerchief. Faith struggled against her tears for the remainder of the service.

Before the singing of the last hymn, Marcus stepped into the pulpit. "I'd like to take a minute of your time before you leave to make an announcement. I will be leaving Blessed Mother as of this afternoon."

There were whispers about the room and the soft buzz of conversation. Faith heard the low timbre of Ben's voice as he turned to his wife and spoke, but she couldn't make out any of his words.

Marcus continued, "I want to say that you have..."

To the surprise of many and Marcus in particular, an elegantly dressed, elderly lady, three rows ahead of Faith and the Halls, rose with the aid of her cane until she stood erect. "I haven't heard a word about this, Father Marcus. Where are you going?"

Marcus looked at a loss for words. He clearly hadn't expected anything like this from the congregation. "I'll be taking a little..."

Father Michael rose and stepped to Marcus' side. "It hasn't been decided definitely where Father Marcus will go, as of today. But it is certain that we will all..."

"I'd like to know why," the old woman persisted. "He's the best parish priest we've had around here in years, aside from you, of course, Michael."

Laura leaned over and whispered in Faith's ear. "That's Millicent Trevor, heir to the Trevor Electronics fortune, and she loves Marcus. She's pretty influential in the church—she's about the biggest benefactor in the parish."

Father Michael looked slightly annoyed. "Point well taken, Millicent, I'm sure we're all going to miss Father Marcus, but we have no choice. He has been called elsewhere. The Mass has ended," he quickly said, "Go in peace to love and serve the Lord."

The parish responded, "Thanks be to God."

Father Michael nodded to the organist who instantly began the introduction to the closing hymn. There was a shuffling sound to Faith's left. She turned and saw that Ben had left their pew and was walking hastily down the side aisle without Kitty. Laura grabbed Faith's wrist again, looked at her and rolled her eyes. "Get ready for a bumpy ride," she said into Faith's ear as the congregation continued to sing. Faith's stomach began to churn.

When Faith, Laura and Kitty left the church, Ben was nowhere in sight.

"I'm so sorry this happened," Kitty began. "He's leaving, isn't he, Laura? He's

leaving the priesthood."

"Yes, Mom. He wanted you to get here last night so he would have some time to talk with Dad, to explain to him why and how he came to his decision."

"Well, you know your father. That would take more than one night. It's going to take some getting used to. You know how he's always felt about Marcus and the priesthood."

"I do, Mom. And sometimes I can't help but wonder why he's so adamant about someone else's life."

Kitty turned to look at her daughter with raised eyebrows. "He's just always felt that way. You know what an honor he considers it."

Laura sighed and let it drop.

They continued walking toward the parking lot where Ben and Kitty had parked. As the neared the car, they saw Ben sitting in the driver's seat with his elbows on the steering wheel. His head was buried in his hands.

Kitty stopped in her tracks. "Let me talk to your father. We'll meet you back at the hotel. We know where it is; we've stayed there before." She turned to Faith. "I'm sorry about this, Faith. Perhaps Laura will explain it to you. I really am so sorry." Kitty hurried over to the passenger side of the car and got in.

From the distance the girls could see that Ben didn't raise his head even when Kitty joined him in the car. "Let's go back into the sanctuary. Marcus wanted us to wait there for him after Mass."

Faith was stunned. She had never seen that side of Ben. Even though she'd never been a parent, she couldn't imagine reacting to your child in this way over a decision that he had obviously agonized over for so long. Though Jillian wasn't her daughter, Faith could never turn her back on the girl even though Jillian had done some pretty despicable things since she had known her.

They went into the church, and Marcus joined them within minutes.

"Did you see him?" Laura asked.

He sighed. "I did. It's what I expected. If only they had come last night. And if Millicent Trevor, bless her crusty old heart, hadn't stood up and voiced her opinion like she did, and Father Michael hadn't jumped in so nervously, he may have only thought I was being transferred elsewhere within the diocese. Then I'd have had a chance to talk to him myself."

They left the sanctuary and went out to Marcus's car. It was a nearly silent ride back to the Foxwood Suites.

Thirty minutes later, Ben and Kitty knocked at their door. All hell broke loose the minute Ben stepped into the room.

"Damn!" he began as soon as the door closed behind him. "Why didn't you talk to me about this before you made that decision, Marcus?"

Faith and Laura rose from the couch simultaneously and started toward the door.

"Stop," Marcus said quietly. "I want you both to stay. This is going to be a civil discussion. No one has to leave." He turned back to Ben. "And I did try to tell you, Dad, several times. You wouldn't listen; you got angry. And you refused to address it again."

Kitty looked nervous. "If Laura needs to leave, let her, Ben. She doesn't need to be upset by this. It was good of Faith to make this trip with her; let them go. I think they'd feel more comfortable somewhere else for now."

Marcus looked at Kitty. "No, Mom. Faith didn't come because Laura asked her. She came because I wanted her to. I wanted the people I care most about to be here with me for my last Mass as Father Marcus."

"My God!" Ben shouted, slamming his fist on the breakfast bar. "So that's it! She's the reason! I never would have expected that of you, young lady!" His face was scarlet. His dark eyes bore into Faith. "And there you were, sitting on the pier with me that day, telling me what a fine man my son was, and all the time you were..."

Kitty cut him off. "Get control of yourself, Ben! You're going to make yourself sick." As she moved toward her husband, her face looked flushed, too. Ben waved her off.

"I'm fine," he said quieting a bit.

"Faith has done nothing wrong!" Marcus' tone was firm but controlled.

Faith turned to Marcus. "I'd like to speak for myself." He nodded.

Faith felt her own cheeks burning as she began. "Let me begin by addressing my statement to you on the pier. And I expect that you'll show me the courtesy of letting me finish what I have to say without interruption." She looked directly at Ben. He was breathing heavily but gave her a slight nod.

"When I said that Marcus was a fine man and that he had helped me through a difficult time, I meant that and nothing more. We had many discussions, mostly while sailing, about my loss of Oliver, the business problems I was facing and the fact that I seemed to have lost communication with God through it all. There was never, for one moment, any intimacy between us during that entire time."

The room was silent. She had everyone's undivided attention. She felt her nerves calming somewhat. The heat began to subside in her cheeks.

"I knew that Marcus had something extremely important troubling him from the first day I met him. But he never talked about himself, and I had no earthly idea what it was. Laura never discussed his business with me either. Marcus and I were two people, with deep problems, who became friends, nothing more. I didn't learn any of the details of this until the day that you, Ben, dropped it on me at the waterside. I can't tell you what a shock that was!" Faith was silent for a moment. "I guess that's mostly what I had to say," a tiny smile crept onto her face as she added, "for now at least."

Marcus nodded at her and gave her a wink of approval.

"Well, maybe I did jump to conclusions that... that I shouldn't have about you, Faith. If I did, I'm sorry," Ben mumbled gruffly.

He had lost some of his steam, but it was clear that he wasn't finished with Marcus yet. "But, Son," he said directing his attention back toward Marcus. He began to pace slowly.

"Oh no, not the pacing," Faith heard Laura mutter under her breath.

"I think you've made this decision far too hastily," Ben was saying. "When I think back over those years growing up when all you ever wanted was to become a priest and now…"

"Dad," Marcus said quietly. "Let's address that, because that's what you always say. In any discussion that anyone has with you about the priesthood, you always say that it was what Marcus always wanted. Well, Dad, Marcus always wanted to please *you*; *that* is the truth. But my becoming a priest was *your* dream for me, not *mine*. What did I study when I went to college? I got my doctorate in Psychology. And in my weakness, because that's what it was, I allowed you to convince me to carry that with me to the seminary. I seriously doubt that you even recognize what you did. But *no* child should be asked to make that kind of sacrifice to please a parent or anyone other than himself.

"It's taken me years of emptiness and discontent to finally come to terms with that fact, to face it head on and address it by making a decision that I could live in peace with. And in doing so, I've grown very strong, Dad."

Kitty took a Kleenex from her pocket. She wiped her eyes then blew her nose. Laura sat like a statue on the sofa, and Faith moved to Marcus' side. He slipped his arm around her shoulders.

"Well, Son…"

"Excuse me, Dad. I wasn't finished."

Ben closed his mouth and sat down on one of the breakfast bar stools.

"I've always loved you, Dad. You were my idol for years. I thought you could do no wrong. And do you know what? I still love you very much. But now I love you with all your warts and flaws, because I see them now. I love you anyway, unconditionally."

Ben had been looking at his son, now he turned away from Marcus.

Marcus reached out to his father. "Look at me, Dad. Please."

His father turned back to him.

"I want you to love me, Marcus Andrew Hall, because of the man I am. I'm no longer Father Marcus, but Marcus Hall is still a good man, Dad. You can't only love me if I fit your mold for me. Because, that isn't love, it's control. There's only one Father who will ever have complete power over me again, and with all respect, Dad, He isn't you. And, I want to be married."

Ben's eyebrows shot up.

Marcus continued. "All of this had been decided before I ever met Faith. When I met her, she was a woman in deep pain, in need of counsel, and I was a man in the same circumstance, but I already knew that I wasn't cut out to live a life that didn't include a wife. We became friends, and that is all! I think you should know me well enough to know that I wouldn't break my vow of celibacy. I've walked away rather than break it. I would have done the same if I'd never met her. But, in knowing her, I've grown to love her very much." He tightened his arm about her. "And now at last, I have the right to pursue my feelings for her. And, she's hearing this for the first time today, just as you are."

Faith knew she was on the verge of tears. What an emotionally charged day this was for her, for all of them.

Kitty blew her nose again. "Marcus, I had no..." she sighed. "I'm so sorry you've been so unhappy, son, if only..." Her words were drowned out by Ben's sobs. He turned and buried his face in his arms on the breakfast bar.

Laura rose and walked to her mother. The two women started toward the hotel room door. Faith leaned up and kissed Marcus' cheek before following Laura and Kitty into the hall.

Outside, the three women walked down the hall and didn't stop until they reached the end of the corridor.

They stood, tears rolling down their cheeks, embracing one another in an intimate huddle, these three most important women in Marcus Halls' life.

It took them several minutes to compose themselves. Kitty was the first to speak. "We picked up the key for our suite on the way up to your room earlier. Let's go down there. I'm sure the men will know where to find us."

Faith and Laura followed her to the suite and waited while she fumbled to unlock the door. Once inside, Faith excused herself and went into the bathroom. She examined herself in the mirror. What a sight she was! Her eyes were red and puffy. Her cheeks were streaked with blusher and mascara, and there was no trace of the lipstick she had applied that morning. She splashed cold water on her face, cupped it in her hands and held it over her eyes. It felt refreshing. Finally, she dried her face and went back into the living room to rejoin Laura and Kitty.

They made small talk, but, as time passed, it was clear from their fidgeting that they were all becoming uneasy. Faith glanced at her watch. "My goodness, it's three-thirty."

Kitty finally voiced what was on all their minds. "Well, I wonder what could be keeping them so long." And then, "Does anyone want any lunch?"

"I'm not hungry," Faith said. "But I could use a cup of coffee."

"Me, too," Laura chimed in.

Kitty stepped over to the kitchenette. "They usually have complimentary coffee with the coffeemaker," she said mostly to herself. "If I can just find where they've hidden the coffee maker."

Just then, all three became aware of a siren. The sound grew louder. Kitty ran to the window and looked out. She turned back to them. "It's coming here!"

At almost the same moment, the phone rang. Laura reached for the receiver. "Hello," she listened... Then, "I will." She returned the receiver to its cradle. Her face was ashen.

CHAPTER 42

Laura turned to Faith and Kitty. "That ambulance is for Dad!"

Laura went to her mother and embraced her. "Dad's alert and talking to Marcus," she said softly, "but he was having some chest pain and taking Tums for it. The pain didn't go away. Marcus called the paramedics as a safety measure." He's going to ride with Dad. He suggested we drive over to the hospital in your car, Mom."

Kitty shook her head and began to cry. "This has been a terrible day. I almost can't believe all that's happened. Your father allows himself to get too upset about things. He's been using a lot of antacids for quite some time now." As she spoke she was opening her handbag and searching for her keys. Finding them, she started for the door,

"Let's go down to the room. Perhaps we can follow the ambulance because I have no idea where the hospital is."

As they reached the room, the paramedics were wheeling Ben, his head partially elevated, out into the hall on a Gurney. A female paramedic supported a bottle of fluids suspended on a pole attached to the stretcher. The I.V. tubing lead from the bottle down into Ben's right arm.

Marcus stepped over to Faith. "Why don't you drive," he suggested quietly. "Mom has a tendency to go to pieces where Dad's concerned. Just put your flashers on and follow the ambulance. We're going to Good Samaritan, about four miles from here."

"I will. Are you alright, Marcus?"

"I'm fine. See you there."

When Ben caught sight of his wife he smiled slightly. He reached out for her hand. "I'm fine. I just had a little indigestion that didn't go away, and Marcus insisted we call these folks. I'm sure they're just going to check me over and..." He stopped mid-sentence and winced. Ben clasped his chest with his free hand. He struggled to catch his breath.

The elevator door opened and they pushed Ben in. As the doors closed,

Faith saw the paramedics hovering over him.

CHAPTER 43

It was a wild ride to Good Samaritan, but Faith managed to stay behind the ambulance. By the time they found a parking place and got into the emergency room, they were told that Ben had been admitted to intensive care. They asked for directions then found an elevator and rode to the fourth floor. As the elevator rose, Kitty began to sob. Laura wrapped her arm around her mother's shoulder.

When they stepped out of the elevator, they saw Marcus standing a distance from them down the corridor to the left. He heard his mother's sobs and started in their direction. They met midway down the hall.

"How is he, dear? It's bad, isn't it?" Kitty was on the verge of hysteria. "What on earth would I do without him?" she asked Marcus.

Marcus wrapped his arms about his mother and pulled her to him. "Now, Mom," he spoke calmly. "We all have to be positive for Dad. And we need to help him by showing him our strength. That's the best thing we can do for him right now. Dr. Nathan Sommers is in there with him. He's a top-notch cardiologist."

"What happened to him after you left us at the hotel?" Laura asked in an unsteady voice.

Marcus answered his sister, as he continued to hold his mother. "Dad's heart stopped. They had to use the defibrillator to get it going again.

Laura looked like a ghost, her eyes moistened. She shook her head slowly. Faith put her arm around Laura's shoulders. She felt teary herself. And, being here, at the hospital, brought back memories of Oliver's stays.

Marcus must have sensed her feelings. He reached out for her hand and gave it a little squeeze. "I think the best thing for everyone would be for you three go back to the motel and try to get some rest. There isn't anything anyone can do here this afternoon. I don't know how long the doctors will be with him, but I'll wait to see what they have to say. I doubt any of us will be able to see him until tomorrow."

"No, dear," Kitty insisted. "I won't leave until I know something. I wouldn't rest if I went back there anyway. No, I'm staying, Marcus." She walked to the end of the hall and went into the waiting room and sat down in one of the chairs.

Marcus turned to Faith. "You and Laura go back. I'll keep in touch by phone. If anything at all changes, I'll let you know. When we're ready to leave, I'll call a cab." He kissed each of them lightly on the forehead.

They had just started for the elevator when they heard the sound of doors opening. A doctor stepped from the intensive care unit into the hall. He began walking toward them. "Are you Marcus Hall?" he asked stopping a few feet in front of them.

"I am. This is Faith Hargrave and my sister Laura."

He nodded at the trio. "I'm Dr. Nathan Sommers. I just left your father. He's alert and coherent. We're giving him some oxygen and fluids, and he's hooked up to some monitors. He's in no pain right now. I'd like for him to get some rest. Tomorrow, if he's up to it, I want to run some tests. He's asked to see you, Marcus. Says you're a priest. I'm going to let you go in briefly. Keep in mind that rest is what he needs right now."

"My mother is at the end of the hall. Will she be able to see him?" Marcus made no attempt to correct the doctor about himself.

"I'm only going to let you go in for now. I'll have a word with Mrs. Hall while you do."

Faith and Laura followed the doctor down to the waiting room as Marcus disappeared behind the doors of the intensive care unit.

Marcus looked about the unit uncertain of which way to proceed. The nurses' station was in the center with cubicles surrounding it. It reminded Marcus of a huge pie, cut in slices, with a large hole cut out of the middle. Every cubicle appeared filled to the brim between the bed and monitoring devices, leaving very little room to navigate about. One of the nurses rose from the station and asked Marcus whom he was there for. He gave her his father's name.

"Right this way," she said. "I was just going to check him again."

Marcus followed her to a space at the far left of the "pie" and waited for her to finish with Ben. As she left, she reminded him to be brief. "No more than five minutes," she had said.

He stepped to his father's bedside. Ben's eyes were closed. Marcus took Ben's right hand between both of his. "Dad, it's Marcus. They gave me five minutes with you."

Ben opened his eyes and nodded. "I have to tell you something," he said weakly. His eyes closed again, and he fell silent.

Marcus continued to hold his father's hand as he waited. Ben opened his eyes a moment later. "I want…" he said then closed his eyes again.

"Dad, you rest. I'll come back later." He felt Ben's grip tighten.

"No! Stay. I want to go to confession."

"But Dad, you know I'm no longer a priest."

"Technically you are, Son. It isn't midnight, yet. The doctor said no visitors. I knew he'd let me see my priest if he wouldn't let anyone else in." He looked at Marcus and winked.

Marcus couldn't suppress a smile. Even critically ill, Ben was still manipulating people to have things his way.

"Anyway, I want to confess. And you're as qualified as any hospital chaplain to hear my confession." He was silent again. The talking had winded him, and he took several deep breaths before resuming. "I confess that I have…"

The nurse peered into the cubicle, "I'm sorry, Mr. Hall, but your son must leave now."

"Leave, hell!" Ben reared up in bed. "He's my priest. I have something to say to him and…" He was becoming agitated.

"Okay, Mr. Hall," she said in a soothing voice. She stepped to the opposite side of the bed that Marcus stood on, reached down and laid her hand on Ben's shoulder. "If you will lie down and stay calm, I'll let him stay here with you." Her voice was soft and her manner was gentle. She smiled at him.

Ben looked up into her face and mellowed. "Thank you," he said a bit meekly. She left them alone.

"Marcus, just in case I don't make it through this, I want to tell you something. I don't have to waste my time asking you to look out for your mother and Laura, because I know you'll do that; you always have. I want to tell you why I've been the way I have about the priesthood all these years. And I want to ask your forgiveness." He stopped to catch his breath again.

"Dad, you don't have to do this. I forgave you long ago."

"I have to do this for me, Marcus. There's something you have to know."

CHAPTER 44

Ben lay silently for a moment, before saying, "No one, not even your mother, knows this. But years ago, before I became an engineer, I entered the seminary."

Ben's words as a complete and total surprise.

Ben continued, "I had wanted it since I was a kid of eight or nine. But, I was asked to leave because I couldn't make the grade. They told me I had too much 'self-importance and insubordination.' That's what they called it, and they said my temper was too hot. They put me on probation, and I tried, but at the end of the period they asked me to leave again." He lay on his back, staring up into Marcus' eyes. "But you… you had everything that I didn't. You were never prideful. You had a kinder nature than I ever had. I guess I just got all mixed up and lost in my ambition for you, because I couldn't do it myself."

"I don't know what to say, Dad. I never had the slightest..."

"Of course you didn't. Like I said, no one knew. My family wasn't about to tell it. They weren't too proud about it, and, besides, it was no one's business. I moved far from where I grew up so it was an easy secret to keep. I'd have carried that to my grave with me if all this hadn't come up. But now, I can't do that. And I couldn't have you feeling in any way responsible for what happened to me today, especially if I don't get past this one."

"I've forgiven you, Dad. As I said, I did that long ago, when I finally came to terms with my life and where I wanted it to go. I forgive you again now. But I would never take the blame for what happened to you today, and I don't mean that to sound callous. Just as I'm responsible for my life and my happiness, you are responsible for yours, Dad. You need to let some of this aggression go, mellow out and enjoy the rest of your life. You've earned the right to stop pushing yourself so hard."

Ben looked at his son very seriously. "You're absolutely right, Marcus. Absolutely right. I raised quite a man in spite of myself."

Marcus looked at his father and smiled. "I'm glad we had this talk, Dad.

And, it will go no further than this room.

Ben pulled Marcus to him and embraced him. Marcus felt the moisture from his father's tears as their cheeks brushed.

CHAPTER 45

The tests that were carried out the following day revealed three blocked arteries around Ben's heart. Doctor Sommers told the family that Ben had been a walking time bomb. On the second day after his admission, he underwent successful triple by-pass surgery. Ten days later he was released from Good Samaritan. His recovery was so remarkable that a week and a half after discharge Dr. Sommers felt that Ben could make the trip to South Carolina to recuperate at the beach house.

Faith had returned ahead of the rest. She had stayed only long enough to know that Ben was out of danger. She needed to get back and try to establish some degree of normalcy in her life. She felt as if her head had been spinning since Oliver's illness began, then there was the trial and everything that happened with it. Just as that became resolved, a new complication entered her life: Marcus. She knew she cared for him, but he had things to work out, and she couldn't be rushed. All this seemed to weigh on her now, making her feel as if her life was orbiting out of her control. She needed to regain dominion over it. With Marcus' mention of marriage, Faith realized that she wasn't ready for a commitment yet. She had to be sure that her feelings for him weren't because he had helped her in her time of tribulation. She needed to be sure that she truly loved him. He'd just made a life altering decision; she needed to know that he was truly in love with her. She couldn't think straight right now and didn't trust herself to make any decisions more serious than what to eat for her next meal. There were even times when she wondered if she might be having a nervous breakdown.

Faith was just beginning to relax a bit when the Halls arrived at their beach home. It was mid-afternoon on Wednesday, and she was out in back of her place doing some planting to help prevent sand erosion. She saw them drive in and waved. She would call them later, when she was finished, to see how Ben had fared the trip by car. They had planned to take at least three days for it. She hadn't talked to anyone since she returned other than to speak briefly with Laura to let her know she had arrived safely and inquire about Ben.

An hour later she gathered up her garden tools and washed them off at the outside water spigot. Then she watered the fresh plantings. She went into the house and left her sandy clothing in the laundry room. She took a shower and put on fresh clothes and makeup. She swept her hair up onto her head and secured it with combs leaving a few wispy golden tendrils to fall softly about her face. She examined herself in the mirror when she was finished. She couldn't even make up her mind whether she wanted to let her hair continue to grow or to have it cut short again as she had worn it for the past several years. She shook her head at her reflection in the mirror.

"You are really a sorry piece of work these days," she told the woman staring back at her.

Though inwardly she felt hesitant to call down to the Halls', she knew she must.

As she reached for the receiver, her phone jangled, startling her and causing her to jump. She lifted the receiver and answered. It was Marcus. Immediately, she felt uneasy, her stomach felt unsettled.

"How did the patient handle the trip?"

"Very well," he told her. "We actually made it easily in two days."

"Give them all my best. Tell them I'll visit in a few days. I want to give everyone time to get settled in."

"Let me take you to dinner tonight, Faith."

"Oh, Marcus, I think not tonight. The last weeks have been difficult, and you've had a long trip and…"

"Please," he interrupted. "Please have dinner with me tonight. I promise we'll make it an early evening. I feel like we need to talk."

This is what she had been dreading. She needed more time right now, but she agreed to go to dinner with him on the promise of making it a short night. And she had known that this situation must be faced sooner or later. She guessed it was going to be sooner.

He called for her at seven. When she opened the door, he stood looking down at her holding a single crimson rose. It was the color of the roses that Oliver had always brought her, her favorite.

"Thank you," she said, taking it from him. "It's beautiful, my favorite color. Did I ever tell you that?"

"I don't think so," he said following her into the living room.

She found a vase for the rose and added some water. She placed it on the glass coffee table. "I'm ready if you are." Why did she feel so uncomfortable with this man she had always been able to talk to about anything?

"Let's go then," he said.

She was dressed in a bright orange turtleneck sweater and white slacks. She picked up her white blazer from the arm of the sofa.

"Let me help you with that," Marcus said, reaching for the blazer. He slipped it around her shoulders as she put her arms in to the sleeves.

His hands rested on her shoulders for just a moment. A thrill shot through her as she looked up at him and smiled.

"Thanks," she said softly as she began to relax.

They rode for some time and talked about Ben's condition. Marcus told her that his father seemed to be trying to affect a change in himself. "He says he wants to smell the roses more; not feel the need to settle everyone's problems for them. Even says he's willing to get some counseling to help him do it if that's what it takes."

"Good for him! I certainly never would have guessed him to be anything other than easy-going and fun-loving," Faith admitted.

"You only saw him at play and not that often. He's promised this before, but I think he means it this time. He's had a real scare. He's finally faced the fact that he's not immortal. He even says no more consulting. I'll have to wait and see on that one, but I think he'll stay down here and take it easy for a few weeks anyway. He's crowding in on seventy and deserves to. God knows Mom has it coming. She's pretty much planned her life around Dad's schedule, with very few exceptions. "
He pulled the car into the parking lot of the Sandpiper restaurant. "I hope you'll like this place. They have excellent seafood, and their steaks are great, too."

When they stepped inside Faith noticed that the small dining room in the distance was dimly lit. There were tables and several small gazebos to accommodate the diners. A hostess greeted them and, being that the restaurant wasn't crowded, they had their choice of either. Marcus asked for a gazebo.

A waiter brought them menus. "Would you care for a before-dinner drink?"

Marcus declined, just water he said, then looked questioningly at Faith.

"I think not tonight. I'd like a glass of unsweetened tea with lemon."

When the young man came back with their beverages, they were ready to order. Faith chose crab cakes and Marcus opted for a T-bone. While they waited for their dinner to arrive, Faith looked across the table at Marcus. Despite all that the last days had presented him with, he looked more rested and contented than she had ever seen him. *He truly is a handsome man,* Faith thought, *by most everyone's standards.* His eyes were deep blue and his sun-streaked, blond hair had just the slightest hint of natural curl that made it appear manageable even under beach conditions. His skin was the golden bronze of summer, even now, in the fall of the year. She thought him magnificent looking tonight. Something stirred in her as she continued to assess him.

It suddenly occurred to her what she was doing. She had tried not to think of him much over the last several days. Now, here she was, studying him as a woman studies a lover and not paying any attention to what he was saying to her. And she didn't want to do that. Why was she feeling the need to pull back now when everything else seemed to be working out. Why was she suddenly feeling so insecure and unsure? Faith was relieved when their food arrived.

When they finished eating they took their tea and went out onto the deck that fronted the ocean. "I have something to say to you Faith. I've waited a long time to be..."

"Marcus, I..."

"Please," He cut in. "Just let me tell you, Faith. I don't want you to feel any pressure. I just want you to know."

She looked at him and nodded.

"I love you, Faith. I think I've loved you for a long time. I didn't admit it to myself when it first started happening. When I came to the beach and spent time with you, I felt this was where I belonged. I've never had that feeling in my entire life. I think that God guided me here to the ocean, at a time when you were here too, to let me know this was what my life should be.

"I believe you care for me, too, but I know what you've been through. I'm ready and willing to give you time, and wings, if you want to use them. But I want you to know that I'm waiting here for you when you're ready to take the next step. I meant what I said to Dad. I want to marry you." He folded his hands, one over the other, and rested them on the table as he concluded.

She reached across to him and covered his hands with hers. "You read me so well. I do need time. Maybe a little space, too. You're a wonderful man, Marcus. Any woman would be blessed to hear their man say to her what you've just said to me. And I care for you, a great deal. But I still have some things to work out. And it's nothing you've done or haven't done. It's just me…all me. In the meantime, I hope we can be dear friends, like we have been. I hope we can sail together and take walks…" She paused, still looking at him.

He nodded. "That's all I can ask. I'll leave it up to you. If you want to go sailing, you have only to ask. We can walk together, the three of us. Laura needs to walk every day. Whenever you want to go with us, just call or come by. You know when we go."

They left shortly after and were back at Faith's home by ten o'clock. He walked with her to her front door.

"Would you like a night cap?" she asked.

"No, it's getting late, I'll take a rain check."

"Thank you for a very comfortable evening."

He looked at her and grinned. "Is that all it was?" he asked, teasingly. "Just very comfortable?"

She smiled. "It was lovely, thank you." She reached up and put her arms around his shoulders. Her lips brushed his cheek lightly. "Good night."

"Good night, Faith," he replied. But he didn't embrace her; nor did he kiss her. When the door closed behind her, Faith gazed through the window in the door to watch as he turned and walked away. He didn't look back. Faith felt empty.

CHAPTER 46

Faith didn't hear from any of the Halls for several days. She made no attempt to contact them either. She spent two days re-establishing business contacts. She was going to have to get busy and make some money. Her available cash reserve was all but depleted, and she certainly didn't want to resort to selling her company stock. Though it was still low, it was beginning to rebound. She was determined to maintain the family's majority interest.

Luck was with her. She was able to set up appointments for the following week with two referrals she received from two different realty firms.

She called Mary Jane and had a long chat. There was a great deal of catching up to do on both sides. Taylor had started child enrichment, which he attended three days a week, and he loved it. The older boys were playing soccer and wanted to know when Faith was coming to watch one of their games. She promised it would be soon.

As their conversation was winding down, Faith told her about Marcus.

Mary Jane said, "So Marcus was a priest but is no longer. Wow! That just blows my mind! I never would have guessed it. I can't wait to tell Jillian. You know, she was quite taken with him."

"Well, maybe there's still a chance for her." Why ever had she even uttered those ridiculous words?

"I doubt she's his cup of tea. I'd say he'd go more for your type, Faith. He's a great guy, isn't he?"

"Yes. Yes, he is, Mary Jane." She got the distinct feeling that Mary Jane was fishing.

"I really liked him. Brad did too."

"It's been so good having this chat with you," Faith said. I've meant to call every day, but I promise I'll do better in the future."

"I'll call you next time, Faith. It'll be soon."

Faith decided to call Jillian, and, to her surprise, she answered. She sounded busy. She told Faith that she was working in Raleigh, doing a sort of internship in the governor's office. She sounded as if she was enjoying the contacts she was making. Faith didn't find that at all surprising. Jillian would graduate in January. Faith found it hard to believe that that much time had passed.

Faith didn't mention Marcus to her, and Jillian didn't bring him up. Though Jillian hadn't really been warm with Faith, she had been civil. Perhaps there was still hope for them to become friends someday.

On Sunday, she walked down to the Halls'. She noticed that Ben and Kitty's car was gone. She wondered if they'd all gone off together but went up to the porch and knocked anyway.

Laura came to the door. She grinned, "Come in stranger. We've missed you."

"I didn't know if I'd find anyone home."

"Mom and Dad went to spend a few days with Uncle Charles and Aunt Jean. They have a few fences to mend," she added with a grin.

The three of them, Faith, Laura and Marcus spent the evening together. They surf fished from their beachfront for an hour and a half. They didn't catch anything but a net with some broken shells and string in it. They talked and laughed just like old times, actually more than they had in the past. Marcus grilled pork chops for their dinner, and afterward they walked to the public pier together. They bought ice cream cones before leaving and by the time they returned home, Faith was chilled and shivering.

Before they reached Faith's, she said, "I have an appointment tomorrow in the late morning and it may take a while, but I'd like to sail in the afternoon if you're not busy, and if it isn't too cold." she added through chattering teeth.

"I'm going to look for some office space in the morning, and I have a one o'clock appointment to look into becoming a deacon in the church. But, when I get back, if you still want to go, it sounds good to me." Marcus and Laura left Faith at her pier and went back to their place. And thus, their habit of walking and sharing dinner most evenings was renewed.

Laura had become very serious about her painting and devoted hours to it daily. Her confidence grew after Faith had sold several of her seascapes. Laura talked with the owner of a local gallery in the early fall and had shown him some of her work. He had been extremely impressed and had kept the two paintings she had taken with her to sell on consignment.

"These will sell! They're wonderful! Your paintings have emotion. I can smell the ocean when I look at them; I can feel the ocean spray on my face. Bring me more!" he had told her.

Laura was thrilled and that, too, had been a catalyst for renewed enthusiasm. "I just can't believe that he, the owner of a gallery, thinks someone would want to pay money for them too," she told Faith.

"Then you sell yourself short. That's what I've been telling you all along.

My clients bought your paintings, not because I brought them to show but because they loved them!"

Laura blushed, and gave Faith a modest smile.

Ben and Kitty returned to the beach, but Ben had only been content to stay for a short while. In early November as the holiday season was upon them, they had gone back to Richmond. Faith signed three contracts and, after a short delay was able to move into the office space she had leased months earlier. Marcus found office space and was in the process of getting licensed with the state as a psychologist.

Three of Laura's paintings sold quickly, and she began to see Bob Prescott, the owner of the art gallery. He was a widower with no children. He took her to dinner, spent time with Laura and Marcus at the beach house and was, with the exception of Faith, Laura's biggest fan.

Laura blossomed under Bob's attentions.

Faith liked Bob from their first meeting. He was steady, hard-working and honest, and it was plain to see that he was very taken with Laura from the start. Faith asked a couple of her realtor friends about him and found he had an excellent reputation as both a businessman and an individual.

One evening, when Faith went down for their evening walk, Marcus wasn't there. "He's gone," Laura said. "He's gone to spend some time in Wilmington. He also mentioned something about looking into a position that he'd been contacted about in Serenity, North Carolina."

"He didn't tell me he was leaving," Faith looked disappointed. "When will he be back?"

"I don't know," Laura said. "He didn't tell me, Faith. He just said he was going to be away for a while."

The sunny day lost its glow for Faith. Not wanting Laura to know how upset this made her feel, she excused herself and went into the bathroom. Why? Why had he gone without saying a word about it to her when everything was so good between them? Was he tired of waiting for her? Didn't he care for her as much as he thought he did? He hadn't touched her since they had their talk that night seven weeks ago at the *Sandpiper*. He hadn't brought the subject up even once since. And now he was gone, without even mentioning to her that he was leaving. And she was sitting here in Laura's bathroom, feeling miserable and already missing him terribly.

CHAPTER 47

Faith collected herself and went back out to the living room. If Laura suspected she had been crying, she didn't let on. She and Laura visited for a short time when there was a knock at the door. Laura went to answer it and returned with Bob at her side. Faith visited with them briefly before excusing herself and though they asked her to stay, she went home. All evening, she found herself wishing the phone would ring. It didn't.

The next time she went to the Halls', Laura answered the door wearing her painter's smock. "Wait here a minute," she told Faith. "I don't want anyone to see this one until it's completed."

"Why? You've let me see all your other work in progress."

"Well, I've been so lucky lately that I, I..." she stammered. "I think I'm getting superstitious. I once read of an artist who never showed his work to anyone until it was completed and he sold every painting. One day, he broke his rule and that painting remained in his personal collection for the rest of his life," she confessed.

Faith laughed and shook her head. *That doesn't make sense at all,* she mused.

Laura disappeared into the den. "Okay," she called a few seconds later. "You can come in now."

When Faith stepped into the den, the painting was draped with a white tablecloth. She laughed. "Whatever works for you, Laura."

"I've decided to go to Richmond for Thanksgiving, Faith. I've asked Bob to go with me because I want him to meet Mom and Dad." She grinned at Faith and blushed like a young schoolgirl with her first boyfriend.

"That's wonderful, Laura. He's becoming very important to you, isn't he?"

"Yes. He is. He's such a wonderful, thoughtful man. And he makes me feel special. I feel so lucky to have met him." Her eyes danced.

Faith hugged her friend. "I'm truly happy for you. You're two very special people."

"Do you want to go with us? I hate to think of you being here alone."

"No. I'll be fine. This is your time. You go and enjoy it. When do you plan to leave?"

"Next Tuesday."

That was four days away. "Have you heard anything from Marcus?" Faith asked, trying to sound casual.

"Not a word."

"Will he be in Richmond for Thanksgiving?"

"I have no idea," Laura replied.

When Laura and Bob left for Virginia on Tuesday morning, Faith still hadn't heard anything from Marcus. He'd been gone for a week. She felt lonely and miserable even while Laura was home. Mary Jane called her twice and invited her to join them for Thanksgiving dinner both times. She declined the invitations. She felt herself backsliding. Her mood was becoming increasingly darker.

Faith didn't leave her house all day Tuesday. She had only one phone call, and that was a wrong number. On Wednesday evening, she walked to the public pier alone.

Thanksgiving was gloomy, very chilly and overcast until late afternoon. Faith lazed around the house all day. Half-heartedly, she took a Stouffer's turkey dinner out of the freezer and opened a can of chilled cranberry sauce for her evening meal. After she threw her foil plate away and stored the leftover cranberries, she started out for her evening trek to the pier.

Even dressed in layers and a warm-up suit, the wind chilled her, but she continued on. When she reached the pier, she walked out to the end and climbed to the observation level as she had so many times before. She sat gazing out beyond the white caps toward the horizon. The orange sun was little more than a fading glow in the distance as she stared beyond the sea focusing on nothing. She felt the wind whip at her face and sting her cheeks. She lifted her hand to her face and felt moisture. Was it tears or only ocean spray? She couldn't tell. She thought back over Oliver's last letter to her. He wanted her to go on. He wanted her to live fully and enjoy life for both of them. He wanted her to feel no guilt in being happy again. And right now, she didn't think she could be much unhappier. Why? Suddenly she admitted to herself why. She was reluctant to follow her heart and love again, because she was afraid to face losing great love for a second time.

She sat there until the full moon appeared in the sky. It would light her way back. She stood and retraced her steps to the entrance of the pier. There were only three others on the pier at this hour... all men... all of them fishing. She started toward home; a lone figure treading slowly through the sand in the moonlight.

What's wrong with me? She wondered as she walked. *Where am I headed? Why am I such a coward? I've already done the very thing I've been afraid of. I've lost the man I love again. And **I** did it, this time. No one took him from me; I drove him away myself.* She continued on for twenty-five minutes, feeling cold, lonely and desolate. As she neared the Halls' beach home, she looked up at the moon. It looked like one of Laura's paintings. It was gorgeous, nearly full, with billowing, translucent clouds drifting across it.

She took a few more steps before she noticed a man coming toward her. As he came closer, her pulse quickened. His hair looked almost silver in the moonlight. He was tall with broad shoulders, a trim waist and long legs. His pace quickened as he neared her. This time there was no mistaking him for Oliver. She felt unnerved, her knees were weak, she was trembling. Marcus reached her, and she fell into his embrace.

"Oh, Marcus! Marcus." she sobbed. "I love you, I love you so much." Her voice became a whisper. She looked up at him. "I've been miserable ever since you left. I've been so…"

His lips covered hers. He pulled her against him so tightly that she almost lost her breath. It felt wonderful! She snuggled against him; she didn't want him to ever release her.

When he finally did loosen his hold on her, he looked down into her eyes. "I've missed you, too, so very much. I gave you time, and it didn't seem to make a difference.

So, I tried giving you some space. Laura said she thought you were ready, that she thought you …"

This time her lips stifled his words. She felt as if she had been dead for a very long time, and now she was alive again. And, it was a most marvelous feeling!

A little later, they walked on to his place. "I don't ever want to be away from you again, Marcus," she told him, as they reached his steps.

"Come in. There's something I want to show you."

Faith followed him up the stairs to the porch and on into the den. She watched as he walked over to Laura's easel. She saw him reach for the tablecloth that covered the painting.

"Laura doesn't want anyone to look at that," she told him. "It isn't finished."

"Yes, it is."

She drew in her breath as he removed the covering to reveal a painting of a man and a woman standing on the shore, at sunset, looking out at the ocean. The man was tall, his hair was sun-streaked-blond, and he was very handsome. He looked like Marcus. The woman was tall, slender and blond. She was leaning with her back against the man's chest. His arms encircled her; her hands rested on his. They looked completely happy and at peace.

"Why, it *is* finished!" She stepped closer to the picture. "It's beautiful; her best yet." She looked back at him and smiled. "And best of all, it's us," she said softly.

Marcus stepped behind her and wrapped his arms around her. "It's actually been finished for some time. And now, everything about it is right. Laura painted this for us in the early fall. It's to be her wedding gift to us."

"It's the perfect gift," she whispered."

Faith turned in the embrace of the man she knew she would love for the rest of her life. She felt complete again. Her belief had been restored, even strengthened, and she had discovered that she was capable of loving deeply again. And, in the process, she had grown in wisdom.

Finding Faith had been an amazing journey.

LaVergne, TN USA
24 January 2010
170997LV00002B/48/P